COPPER EVENING

A NOVEL

STUART FABE

Author's Note

UNTIL RECENTLY I'd never heard of the Keweenaw Peninsula which is located in the northernmost part of the Upper Peninsula of Michigan. In my search for dark places to photograph the night sky, I learned about Brockway Mountain and the reasons why this historic region along the southern shore of Lake Superior is known as "copper country."

With additional research and my subsequent visit to this area, I learned how Paleo-Indians, principally Chippewas, dug and collected copper ore thousands of years before white Europeans arrived. They heated and hammered the mineral into utensils, and implements for hunting and fishing, and for ceremonial objects and jewelry.

I also became intrigued by the number of immigrants, including several hundred thousand from Finland, who ventured to the Keweenaw to find

a better life beginning in the 1840s. Many of their proud descendants remain to this day.

What the immigrant miners often found instead was an equally harsh existence from what they'd left behind. Working deep underground to extract millions of pounds of copper for investors, and with harsh winters that annually dumped three hundred inches of snow, the workers' dreams sometimes turned into nightmares.

Over the years numerous copper mines experienced serious labor disputes. Several mines became consolidated to survive, only to see their ore eventually depleted. Mining villages like Allouez, Kearsage, Delaware, Phoenix, Mohawk, and Mandan became ghost towns.

Today, the Keweenaw Peninsula boasts a population of some forty thousand hardy souls. Places like the Quincy Mine near Hancock are available for tours, and the history of the copper country has become legendary, thanks to the respectful stewardship and support from dedicated organizations like the National Park Service and the Quincy Mine Hoist Association.

Copper Evening is the fifth story in my Clay Arnold series and is set in the Keweenaw Peninsula. With a dramatic background of ancient Indians, ghost towns, lighthouses, Lake Superior, and copper mines over nine thousand feet deep, it became too fascinating a setting for Clay Arnold, and me, to pass up.

Regarding my hero, Clay Arnold, well let's just say that he's continuing to "evolve"as a person. He's a very devoted husband, father, and friend, and his professional photographic skills are in as much demand as ever. However, he still harbors deep, abiding feelings about righting wrongs, especially for those in need. His lethal Demon camera is always nearby, and while he prefers not to use it, he keeps it close at hand nonetheless.

I write all of my stories purely for entertainment. Much of the information is factually accurate, while other details are conjurings of my imagination. Readers of my past novels will recognize some familiar characters, but I always enjoy adding new personalities to the mix. As I've said before, *"Plots are the vehicles on which stories ride. Characters are their pilots and passengers."*

I sincerely hope you enjoy this story and perhaps plan your own visit to learn why the Keweenaw Peninsula has captured my imagination.

Stuart Fabe

Dedication

*To the People of the Keweenaw Peninsula
Whose History is Legendary.*

And

*To Daniel Joseph Hoffheimer
A Treasured Friend.*

~ Prologue ~
The Keweenaw Peninsula
Upper Peninsula of Michigan

Circa AD 1500

A YOUNG TANNED BOY walks along the southern shore of Lake Superior with his wolf pup at his side. The young wolf tugs at its deer-hide leash urging the boy to play. Ahmik is eager to follow his grandmother's instructions, though, to find the copper rocks that are strewn along the water's edge and in pits near their Chippewa village. She will beat and shape the pieces of metal into crude cooking utensils and give chunks of ore to the men to fashion fish hooks and tips for their arrows and spears.

Ahmik stops and stares at the great expanse of water that his tribe calls Gitche Gumee. It's early summer now, and the ice and deep snows have melted revealing the vast waters of this inland

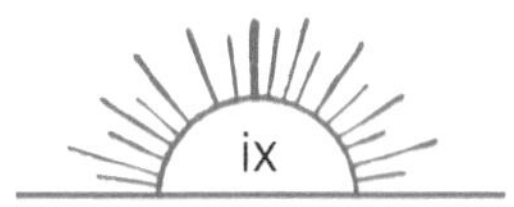

ocean and a forested landscape that has finally shed its shroud of winter whiteness. His eyes squint as he looks into the setting sun, and his face is sprayed by windswept water coming off the deep, dark lake.

"Come, Grey!" he exhorts his wolf pup. "The sun will set soon, and Nokomis has told me to return before dark. We must find more copper rocks and hurry home for tonight's council fire. C'mon my little wolf friend! It'll be night soon, and we don't want the evil spirit, Windigo, to find us in the dark alone."

Ahmik treats his rambunctious pup to pieces of dried fish from his deerskin pouch, and he picks up more pieces of copper and adds them to another pouch that he's strapped to the young wolf's sturdy back. The two friends scrabble their way over shore rocks that have been rounded by the great lake's tumbling wave action. Together they search for the copper ore hoping to please Nokomis with what they bring to her wigwam.

Ahmik stops for another moment, closes his eyes, and listens to the wind in the trees and the sound of the waves just as his father, Red Fox, has taught him to do. He pats Grey on his head and says, "Father has told me that we're all one in the eyes of the Great Spirit, Gitche Manitou. The trees, the land, the water, the fish, all of the plants and animals. Even you and me, Grey."

The wolf pup sniffs the air and extends his paw begging for another fish treat which Ahmik generously offers. The sun is even lower now in the western sky casting long shadows and high-lighting rocks from a different angle than when they started their search for copper. They turn to leave the shoreline and return to the path home. Ahmik casts a final glance at the setting sun and notices a bright, white object shimmering in the day's fading light.

"What's this, Grey?" he whispers to his friend as he approaches the object half-buried in the sandy soil. "Is it a rock? I think not, and I've never seen a clam shell that looks like this before! We should bring it home and see what Nokomis and my parents say."

Ahmik reaches his hand out to grasp the porcelain-like shell, and he feels a source of vital energy unlike anything that he's ever experienced before. He pulls his hand back in apprehension but sees that nothing bad has happened to him. The wolf pup sniffs and yaps a sound of encouragement, and Ahmik reaches for the reflective object again. It shimmers in his hand, and he immediately feels a sense of well-being and peace. He peers closely at his new prize, watching it glow and then places it in his pouch. Even covered in the deer hide he sees a pulsating shimmer from within.

"Come Grey! We've dawdled too long. I can't wait to show grandmother what we've found!" Ahmik finds the path leading to their village, and all the way home both the boy and his wolf pup feel a surge of physical energy.

The path to their village is lined with pines, maples, and white-skinned birch trees. The trees' leaves and needles form a canopy over them blocking out the last lingering vestiges of daylight. In the dim light, Ahmik is fascinated that the white shell he found is glowing even brighter than before. He and Grey quicken their pace, and before long they see their village of some thirty birchbark wigwams populated by their tribe of over a hundred men, women, and children. The wigwams and lodges are nestled between a large pond and a clear, rushing brook. Wild rice grows on the pond's water, and well-tended fields of corn surround the village. This is the only home that Ahmik has known in his seven summers of life.

"Nokomis!" Ahmik calls out as he approaches his grandmother's wigwam. "Nokomis, come see what Grey and I have brought you!"

A few moments later an older, wise-looking woman emerges through the deerskin flap that is the entrance to her wigwam. She is perhaps some sixty years of age, and her long silver hair, her ornately-beaded dress, and ceremonial jewelry give her a regal bearing.

"Ahmik, I was beginning to worry that you would be late for the council fire. And, I see you still have that half-wild beast you call your wolf-friend. Is he well enough behaved now to keep?"

As if on command, Grey approaches Nokomis and buries his face between her knees. He moans happily and wags his tail in enthusiastic circles.

"I suppose so," the older woman laughs as she scratches behind the wolf pup's ears. "I guess we won't have to eat you after all, huh?!"

Ahmik smiles as he sees his wolf-friend win his grandmother's affection.

"So show me, Ahmik, show me what I asked you to bring, and we must not take long because the council fire will begin when the moon rises in the east."

Ahmik bends down and releases the hide pouch that he'd fastened on Grey's back, and the young wolf shakes his fur and prances with his refound liberation. Ahmik empties the contents of the pouch onto the ground by their feet, and Nokomis stoops down to inspect the copper rocks her grandson has brought.

"Ah, you've done very well, Ahmik. These are nice pieces that the other women and I'll be able to use, and I'll give several to the men for their hunting needs. Thank you, Ahmik." She hugs the young boy, and Grey spins in a circle of delight.

"Come now, Ahmik, we must get you something to eat and then hurry to the council fire. Chief Sakima wishes to tell the migration story and the visions of the prophets. He'll not be pleased if we arrive late."

"Of course, Nokomis, but there is something else that Grey and I've found, but I don't know what it is. It's not like any other shell that I've seen before, and it seems to have a spirit-force of its own. I was hoping you could tell me what it is."

"Show me, Ahmik," Nokomis replies dubiously. "Then, let's get you and this little beast something to eat."

Ahmik removes the straps of his deer-hide pouch from his breechcloth and lays it on the ground. The pouch's contents shimmer and glow brightly, and Ahmik pulls out the unique shell and lays it on the pouch. It glows white in the dusky light, and Nokomis gets on her aged knees to inspect the object more closely. A look of astonishment seizes her face, and Ahmik sees the glowing shell reflected in his grandmother's eyes.

"Where did you get this, Ahmik? Did anyone else see you find it?"

"Grey and I found it half-buried in the sand on the rocky shore near the entrance to the path that leads home. We didn't see any others like it, and no one else was around. It was getting dark, and you warned me to be home so the evil spirit, Windigo, wouldn't eat me. What is it, and why does it shimmer?"

"Very good questions, my grandson. I have heard stories of such a shell, but I want to show it to our chief and medicine men. Take these pieces of copper and go inside my wigwam and get something to eat. You'll find deer meat, corn, beans, and squash. I'll take your shimmering shell to Chief Sakima and meet you and your parents at the council fire."

"Thank you, Nokomis, and thank you for sharing your food. Grey and I will be along shortly."

By the time Ahmik arrives at the council fire, most of the tribe has assembled and is seated around the large blaze. Ahmik's parents have saved room for him and his wolf pup in the middle of the group, close enough for them to hear the chief and be warmed by the fire. Nokomis will sit with them as well, but she's involved in a very serious conversation with Sakima.

Ahmik sees Nokomis point him out to the chief, and his parents wonder what that is all about.

"Did you misbehave while your mother and I were fishing and collecting berries, Ahmik? Why is your grandmother pointing you out to the chief?"

"I don't know, father. Grey and I collected copper for Nokomis as daylight came to an end, and I found a peculiar shell that grandmother wanted to show the chief. That's all I know."

Just then Nokomis and the chief end their conversation, and she comes to sit with the family.

"What was that about, Nokomis? And why is the chief interested in Ahmik?" the boy's father asks.

Nokomis is about to reply when Sakima, chief of the Chippewa people, stands to address the tribe. Nokomis holds her hand up to silence Ahmik's father. "Listen and learn!" she intones knowingly. "There is much to hear!"

And the chief begins, "We are Chippewas!" Sakima declares proudly to his tribe. "We are descendants of the Anishinaabe, the original people! Tonight I stand before you to recount the visions of our prophets, and to bring you exciting news — and some serious concerns."

The chief paces thoughtfully before his people, and the bonfire crackles as he tosses a pine log onto the pyre dramatically sending sparks flying into the night sky.

"Many of you have heard our Midewin medicine men and me speak in the past of the prophesies that have guided our existence. For our young people, and all of us, it is time to speak of the prophesies again. Many, many seasons ago our people lived on the shores of a great salt water. The prophets instructed our people to follow a sacred Megis shell into the west until they reached a place where food grew upon the water. The prophet warned that if they did not do this that they would be destroyed.

"Another prophet told our people that they would eventually be camped by a large body of water. He also foretold that in this time the sacred Megis shell would be lost and the Midewin, our medicine men, would subsequently diminish in strength. He gave hope though because he had a vision that a boy would be born who would point the way back to our traditional ways and to the future of our Chippewa people."

Sakima pauses momentarily as he looks into the faces of his people. He searches for the proper words and solemnly begins again. "Yet, another prophet told of the coming of a Light-Skinned race. The prophet said, 'You will know the future of our people by the face the Light-Skinned race wears. If they come wearing the face of brotherhood, then there will come a time of wonderful change for generations to come. They will bring new knowledge and in this way two nations will join to make a mighty nation. You will know the face of brotherhood if the Light-Skinned race comes carrying no weapons. If they come bearing only their knowledge and a hand shake.

"But then the prophet said, 'Beware if the Light-Skinned race comes wearing the face of death. You must be careful because the face of brotherhood and the face of death look very much alike. If they come carrying a weapon … beware. Their hearts may be filled with greed for the riches of this land. If they are indeed your brothers, let them prove it. Do not accept them in total trust. You shall know that the face they wear is one of death if the rivers run with poison and the fish become unfit to eat. You shall know them by these many things.'"

Sakima pauses again and looks upon his assembled people. He hears their murmurs and sees their heads nodding, acknowledging the warnings. He tosses another dry pine log onto the pyre sending a burst of sparks and flames into the night sky. He raises his hand to silence the assemblage, and he begins again.

"The prophet warned, 'There will come a time of great struggle that will grip the lives of all Chippewa people. There will come false prophets among the people who hold promises of great joy and salvation. If the people accept these promises of a new way and abandon the old teachings, then great struggle will be with the people for many generations. The promises that come will prove to be false promises. All those who accept these promises will cause the near destruction of the people.'"

Now the tribe's murmurs turn to shouts of indignation. "No! This shall not be!" shouts a voice from the crowd. "We will repel the Light-Skinned race and save our way of life from these evil ones!"

Sakima waits patiently for members of his tribe to vent their fear and rage. He wants the gravity of the prophesies to fully sink in. Ahmik leans against Red Fox for comfort, and Meadow Dew lightly strokes his head. Nokomis stoically stares straight ahead into the blazing council fire.

"Silence!" the chief bellows, and the tribe's shouts of righteous indignation ebb into simmering murmurs until only the sound of the roaring bonfire can be heard.

"We are the descendants of those ancient forbearers. We have made the great migration to the large body of water, Gitche Gumee. We harvest rice from the water just as the prophesies have said. But — the sacred Megis shell, with all of its spirit powers for preserving life, has been lost to us and the healing powers of our tribal healers, have been diminished — that is, until today!"

The chief strides into the midst of the assembled tribe and pulls out the sacred Megis shell that Ahmik and Grey found on the beach and holds it up for all to see. It shimmers and glows with a preternatural whiteness that outshines even the brightness of the bonfire.

"Behold! The Megis shell has been found!"

Voices of surprise and reverence rise among the tribe, and even the Midewin healers in the crowd are stupefied by what they see and begin chanting incantations understandable only to themselves.

"There's more!" Chief Sakima states firmly. "Where is the boy named Ahmik, son to Red Fox and Meadow Dew and grandson to Nokomis? Stand and be recognized!"

Ahmik tries to bury his embarrassed face in his mother's tunic, but his father draws him away and instructs him to stand. He looks into his parents' eyes plaintively for support and then stands for all to see.

"As the prophesies have also foretold, a boy has come to lead us back to our traditional ways. Ahmik found the sacred Megis shell, and in so doing he has secured our destiny and the restorative powers of our medicine men!"

A great din arises around the council fire, and Chief Sakima presents the sacred Megis shell to Ahmik. Unable to hide from the attention the chief has directed on him, Ahmik accepts the sacred shell and immediately feels a charge of energy shoot into his very being. His shyness is transformed into an abiding spirit of responsibility for his people, and he holds the Megis shell up to the heavens. His parents and Nokomis look on in stunned admiration, and the medicine men bow their heads in respectful adulation.

"Beginning this very evening," Sakima declares, "I will meet with our Midewin healers and Ahmik. Our goal will be to reestablish the tradition of learning the secrets of the Megis shell, and to seek ways to ensure a lasting line of medicine men who know the paths to spiritual living and physical longevity. And yes, these practitioners, this Grand Medicine Society, will protect what was given to us by the great spirit, Manitou, and our Anishinaabe ancestors. If and when the Light-Skinned race arrives, friend or foe, our way of life will be never be lost again!"

Sakima concludes his speech and commands that a great feast be brought for the people. The tribe rises euphorically from the council fire and scatters about bringing food and musical instruments. Akmik and Grey are fascinated by the spectacle that his tribe is creating. Chanting, drumming, and dancing lasts late into the night, and when the council fire finally burns low everyone eventually withdraws to their wigwams. Once again there is quiet in the village. Then, the chief approaches and speaks solemnly with Ahmik's parents and Nokomis.

"Your son does not yet know how special he is or how important his finding the Megis shell is to our Chippewa people. I have spoken with our Midewin medicine men, and they will take him and the sacred shell to a secret holy place on the great mountain further inland, and there they will all relearn the paths to healthy spiritual living and long life, perhaps immortality itself. And, they will prepare for a long lineage of Midewin healers who follow in their footsteps and protect the energy of the Megis shell and the secrets of its ways. At long last the visions of the ancient prophets will be fulfilled."

Ahmik cannot believe what he is hearing. He is proud to be chosen and yet fearful and humbled by what he does not know. He pulls Grey close to him for support. "My wolf-friend can come too, yes?!" he beseeches, and the chief voices his agreement. His parents vacantly nod their understanding to Sakima, although neither of them can fully comprehend the gravitas of the situation. Nokomis smiles knowingly, warmly hugs Ahmik, whispers private words of encouragement to him, and quietly walks away.

The next morning dawns brightly, and the winds off the great lake carry a spirit of fresh hope for the future of the Chippewa people, but Ahmik, Grey, the Midewin healers, and the sacred Megis shell are now gone from their village nestled along the shores of Gitche Gumee.

Chapter 1

Present Day

SOMETIMES WONDER HOW I ever got so lucky. I mean, I'm not lucky all of the time, you know, like winning lotteries and things like that, but as I look around our dining table at the faces of family and friends, I feel very fortunate indeed.

First and foremost is my ever-adorable wife, Maggie, who helps put me in touch with my kinder self, and who also puts me in my place when I need

it. Maggie continues to run her public relations business, although she's drastically cut back her workload to include only a few special, long-term clients. She's decided that chasing fame and fortune isn't as important as it once was, and she's happiest when she's here with Tori and Mace and me, of course. We've been very happily married for fifteen years now, and our fourteen-year-old son, Bodie, and his brother, Rennie, bring us joy beyond words.

My lifelong friend, Tori Rawlins, is seated next to Maggie and is like a sister to me. Tori has been blind since birth, and her twin brother, Weed, was like my own brother. We grew up together just a few houses apart, and our lives have been intertwined ever since. Sadly, Weed had his life tragically snuffed out by a henchman's bullet when we were on a hunt for Samuel Morse's art treasure many years ago now. It has taken me a long time to keep from tearing up whenever I look at Tori because of Weed. I've always blamed myself for his death although nobody else seems to. Thank goodness we all look after each other.

Then there's Mace! On the surface we are very different, but despite his being in his late eighties and an older black man, I care about Mace as much as any person on the planet. His wisdom, knowledge, and good heart have been inspirational to me. That plus the fact that he's literally saved my ass on more than one occasion are reasons enough for my devotion to him.

Mace has lived on the grounds of this renovated, nineteenth-century beer brewery complex that I own since he came here as a sixteen-year-old kid from the Bahamas looking for work. After the original beer brewery closed, it became the Jeffries Woodworking Mill, and Mace stayed on. In fact, when old man Jeffries sold me the complex some twenty years ago, his only indelible proviso was that Mace Davis be allowed to live in the power plant as long as he chose. I agreed, and it was one of the best decisions I've ever made. He's been living here along the White River a little north of Indianapolis ever since and keeps a very cozy home in our old power plant across the courtyard.

Truth is, I couldn't run this place without Mace. He and Satchmo the cat know this place better than anyone ever could. I'm also very fortunate that Mace has become an expert curator of my antique camera museum attached to Maggie's and my home in the old brewery building. I think his giving tours to school groups and collectors has been a large reason for his feet hitting the floor in the morning. He loves talking about the old cameras in the collection, and he's become very good at it. Like I said, I'm lucky.

Before Rennie went off to college, he bunked with Mace and our now-gone dog, Lex. Lex was a wonderful black Labrador who managed to get around on only three legs after he was shot by a couple of jerks who attacked Tori and Rennie as they hiked along the White River several years ago. Now it's just Mace living in the power plant, and he keeps our entire property running like a well-oiled machine. I don't even want to think of his eventual demise, but it's clear that time is beginning to take its toll on him. It'll be beyond heartbreaking for all of us when he eventually goes.

And, of course there's Satchmo who's asleep on Mace's lap. Satchmo is the largest darn Maine Coon cat that you ever saw and a one-cat tour de force when it comes to keeping the brewery complex free of rodents. Given his advanced age, Satchmo probably isn't long for this world, but I wouldn't bet against the old cat living forever either. He's one tough pussycat!

Not everyone is with us tonight. Bodie is enjoying another summer as a camper at Camp Voyager on Lake Winneboujou near Brule, Wisconsin. He's as bodacious as ever, and Maggie and I marvel at how nicely he's maturing. That's not to say that he doesn't do some boneheaded things occasionally, but what the hey, I still do too.

Happily, Bodie is one resilient kid. We don't often talk about that time five years ago when he and President Jacob Horvath got kidnapped by nasty Russian agents while fly fishing on the Brule River, but we don't shy away from the conversation when it comes up either. Something like that could scar a kid for life, but he seems to be fine. Hell, he saved the president's life and helped defuse a global conflagration. Jake Horvath is alive because of my son, and neither of them will ever forget what they endured together and the friendship that they forged. That'll make a father bust his buttons with pride! Alas, Maggie still cringes and shakes her head in maternal disbelief at the thought of that terrifying episode.

Our adopted son, Rennie Cotton, is doing a summer internship with the National Park Service in Calumet, Michigan, fulfilling some field work as part of his doctoral program in Sociology. Pretty amazing that a homeless black kid who Mace and I plucked off the mean streets of Indianapolis over twenty years ago would ever go to college at Northwestern let alone be well on his way to earning a PhD. Nature versus nurture?! You decide. One thing's for sure. Rennie never could've achieved what he has without the collective efforts and love from everyone sitting around this table. On the other hand none of us would be the people we are without having Rennie in our lives. His presence has been transformative, and we all love Rennie and Bodie to the moon and back.

And then, I guess, there's me. My name's Clay Arnold, and aside from having devoted relationships with all of the aforementioned folks in our family of friends, I'm a photographer of some note. Okay, some people in the art world would say that "some note" doesn't quite describe the impact and popularity of my photography, but I still think of myself as a photographer who just enjoys shooting the world as I see it. I'm glad that people seem to appreciate my body of work.

But, like many people I have a personal history that very few folks know anything about. While I've gotten a lot of the anger that I feel for right-wing racists and criminals who prey upon vulnerable people out of my system, I know that I'm still capable of exacting harsh vigilante justice on thugs who I deem deserving. I won't go into chapter and verse about the executions I've committed, and thankfully I've evolved somewhat since becoming a husband and father, but I still stay armed with lethal devices like my antique Demon camera that Mace and Weed modified for me years ago. I've learned that it's a dangerous world out there, and if push comes to shove, especially involving my family, I'm not going down quietly. Just sayin'.

Just then the phone rings, and I see that it's Rennie calling us from his newly rented apartment in Calumet, Michigan. "Well, this is a nice surprise!" I tell Rennie. "Have you gotten yourself pretty well situated in your new place on the Keweenaw Peninsula for the summer?" Everyone around the table stops talking so they can eavesdrop on our phone conversation.

"Hi Dad, yeah, I found myself a nicely furnished place not far from where I'm working at the National Park Service office. My job started a few days ago, so I wanted to touch base with everyone at home before my life gets too hectic."

"So, what'll your job responsibilities entail, and how do you like the people you're working with?"

"Everyone seems very nice here, and the NPS staff are super dedicated to preserving and inter-preting the history of this region they call 'Copper Country.' I've been assigned to work with the educa-tion ranger named Kelli Katterman, and from what I can tell so far, I think selecting the Keweenaw Peninsula was an excellent choice for my studying early Paleo-Indians and the area's history involving copper mining and logging. As to what my exact job responsibilities will be, Ranger Kelli told me that something very unusual has just been revealed on Brockway Mountain near where the now defunct Brockway Mining Company used to operate. She's asked me to stay flexible until the park service and the local tribal council have an opportunity to discuss whatever it is more closely. I'm hoping I can be involved in researching this new find."

"Sounds pretty interesting, Rennie. I hope this experience turns out to be everything you want. Any idea what they found?"

"No, not really, Dad, the higher-ups are keeping pretty tight-lipped about it, but apparently it's an important artifact that the local Chippewa Indians have been safeguarding for hundreds of years, and they're now thinking about going public with it."

"Any idea why the Chippewa are going public with it now?"

"Not really," Rennie replies, "but yesterday I overheard Kelli's supervisor say some mumbo jumbo about this relic supposedly having mystical healing powers. Apparently, the tribal leaders are arguing among themselves about whether to share this with the outside world. I sure hope they do especially since I'm thinking of proposing to my academic advisor that I write my doctoral thesis on the historical interaction between white European cultures and the indigenous peoples in the Lake Superior area. It'll be fascinating to see what happens if the local Chippewa people really have a secret knowledge that white people need and want. Hopefully, the races will be able to find common ground, but if history is any indication, it could turn ugly. In any event I've got a feeling that there's a lot of things to learn here given the history of ancient Indians, copper mines, ghost towns, and who knows what else! I'm pretty stoked about being here, and I enjoy working with Ranger Kelli."

Rennie pauses a moment and says, "Uh, Dad, let me talk with mom and Tori and Mace a little bit, and then I'd like to talk with you about something else before we all hang up, okay?"

"Sure," I reply wondering if he needs some extra cash or if he's knocked up the tribal princess or something. I hand the phone to Maggie and ask her to give it back to me when everyone's done talking.

Maggie and Rennie talk for a few moments, mainly about if he's eating properly, and if he's living in a safe neighborhood. I can't help but smile when I hear the tone of her voice and the types of questions she's asking Rennie. Sounds pretty similar to how she spoke with Bodie when we were getting him packed up for Camp Voyager. Only thing is there's ten years between their ages. Maggie's great, and our sons will always be boys to her.

Maggie passes the phone to Tori and then Mace as they each get their phone time with Rennie. He only left a few days ago so there's not a lot of stuff for them to report from home. Rennie tells them how the temperature's a lot cooler up on the Keweenaw compared to Indiana, and that he's visited Lake Superior once and couldn't believe how big it is. They each talk for a little bit longer, and then Mace hands the phone back to me.

I walk out to our deck and ask Rennie, "What's up?! Are you okay?"

"Yeah, yeah, Dad, everything's cool. I just wanted to ask you something."

"Shoot!"

"So, there's really a lot of excitement brewing around here about this mysterious Indian artifact, and apparently there's a lot of talking going on about how to present this thing to the world if the Chippewa tribe agrees. They don't want a huge media circus going on with a gazillion reporters and curiosity seekers descending on the peninsula."

"And?" I ask.

"So, anyway, I got all excited and wanted to be helpful, and I told everyone that Clay Arnold is my father and that you might be willing to photograph the unveiling of the artifact by the tribal council. I know I should've spoken with you first, Dad, but I guess I was trying to impress them. I'm sorry."

I exhale and say, "You don't have to apologize, Rennie. I get it, and I suppose there's no way that Ranger Kelli isn't young and pretty too, huh?!"

"Now Dad, you know I'm strictly business here, right?"

"Right," I deadpan, "and your Uncle Weed didn't like looking at ladies' figures either, huh?" I pause a moment and then ask, "When would you want me to come up?"

"Seriously!" Rennie blurts. "You really think you could do it?!"

"I leave for a photographic assignment in a couple of days to Sleeping Bear Dunes near Empire and Glen Arbor, Michigan. It'll be a brief follow-up publicity shoot for their tourist bureau, and I also want to shoot the Milky Way and the night sky over the sand dunes for myself. I figure it's probably about an eight-hour drive from there to Calumet. What if I came about six days from now? Think that might work?"

"Fantastic! That would be great, Dad! Obviously, I'm not in a position to know whether the tribal leaders and the park service folks will get their heads together on this, but having the world-famous Clay Arnold come to do the photography might even help seal the deal."

"All right, then. You know I'm a sucker for flattery," I tease. "Plus, this ancient artifact really sounds pretty fascinating, and if I can help your budding career, I'm very happy to do it. And if it doesn't work out, I can always find something to amuse myself with up there for a couple of days. Of course, I need to clear this with your mother too, but she should be okay, especially with Bodie off at camp."

"This is great, Dad! Thanks! My place has a den with a spare bed so you should be comfortable. This is so cool that you're coming! So, I'll see you in six days, yeah?"

"Yeah, six days, Rennie," I reply with a chuckle, and then we hang up.

I rejoin Maggie, Tori, and Mace at the dining table and hear Mace softly snoring with his chin on his chest and Satchmo still sleeping on his lap.

"So?!" Maggie asks. "What else did Rennie have to say?"

"After my photo shoot at the dunes in a few days, I'm driving up to join him on the Keweenaw Peninsula. I agreed to help him and the park service with a little photography if things work out."

"Well, that's awfully nice," Tori says. "Great way for you guys to bond some more. I remember when you two went out to Dead Horse Point in Utah together. Been a while since it's just been the two of you on the road together."

"Yeah, it has been and please don't remind me about Dead Horse Point. That's where Rennie saved a little girl from plunging over a thousand-foot cliff. We came very close to losing them both."

"Gee, Clay!" Maggie chimes in. "That was before we got married, but I don't seem to recall your ever sharing that insignificant bit of family history with me," she offers sarcastically. "Hmmm, dear?"

"Must've slipped my mind, darling," I reply with a weak smile. "Anyway, so I'll be gone a little longer than I originally thought."

"Not a problem. We've got the home front covered, Clay," Tori says. "So, go and enjoy!"

"But no unnecessary drama, right, sweetheart?" Maggie chimes in knowing my penchant for getting involved in major shitstorms.

"Of course not, darling, what could possibly go wrong?" I regret saying those last words as soon as they leave my mouth. She gives me her all-knowing look, and I flick some imaginary lint off my lapel. Like I said earlier, "I sometimes wonder how I ever got so lucky."

Chapter 2

Rex Trammer stares intently at a medical report sitting on his office desk. It contains the results of his recent oncology exam at the Mayo Clinic. At age seventy three he appears physically fit, but he knows the Glioblastoma Multiforme tumor that his doctors just found in his brain is a death sentence. He's got maybe a year left to live, and the last few months will not be pretty.

He gets up from his desk and walks over to his window overlooking the grounds of the defunct Brockway Mining Company. The old copper mine has been in his family since the 1840s, and although no ore has been extracted from the mine since the mid-1960s, he still owns all of the land and has respected his late father's directives to never sell it. Rex's office is situated atop the mine's number two shaft building some seventy feet above the ground, and from there he can see the remnants of several old stone boiler house buildings, an old steam loco-motive engine, and what was once the largest steam hoist building in the world. A tear flows down Rex's cheek as he quietly laments the demise of Brockway's copper mining operations that used to be envy of the world. That and his devastating cancer report. He knows his great wealth and influence probably can't save him.

A knock on his office door breaks his trance-like stare. He wipes the tear from his cheek and shouts, "Come!"

A moment later the office door swings open, and Rex's operations manager, Digger Finn, walks into the spacious office.

"G'morning, boss!" Digger says. "How're you feeling today?"

"Not bad I guess for a dead man walking," Rex replies bluntly.

Digger nods his understanding but doesn't immediately reply. He has served as Rex's number two man for many years, and even though they're good friends, Digger has learned when to speak and when to be quiet. Aside from his boss, he's the last full-time employee working at the Brockway Mining Company. His duties these days entail supervising a few part-time people who maintain the company's grounds, running the mine's gift shop that is open to the public, and giving underground tours in the mine's seventh level.

"What's the good word, Digger? I could use some good news."

"A couple of things," he replies. "I ran the tally of last month's sales in the gift shop, and we brought in nearly six thousand dollars. That's a good month for us. That also includes fees for tours of the mine and the steam hoist building."

Rex nods his head signifying he's okay with that figure. "What else?" he asks.

"I have a tour this morning at eleven o'clock for seventeen people, and two others scheduled for tomorrow at eleven and three o'clock."

Rex stares out the window again and says to Digger, "Hard to believe that Brockway used to be the largest copper mine in the world, employing thousands of men. Our main shaft went down on an angle for over nine thousand feet. Over six thousand feet in final shaft depth. Well over a mile down! Over ninety levels and all of it below level seven is flooded. Now, we sell a few trinkets in the gift shop and give tours to school kids and tourists. Hard to believe. I'm glad my father isn't around to see it. I guess I won't be for long either."

Digger softly says, "Yeah," as he looks at the floor. He knows that Rex doesn't need him to say anything more.

"Well Digger, if there's nothing else then, I think I'll rest a bit."

Digger turns to leave but stops. He turns around and faces his boss and says, "Rex, there is something else, but I'm reluctant to bring it up to you." He has an awkward expression on his face.

"Oh?" Rex replies. "What is it?"

"I know you're a very private man, and I sure don't mean to invade your privacy, but I heard a rumor about something, something weird that got my attention. Then, I went and checked it out. I think it's something you might want to know about."

Rex walks over to Digger. "Don't you think we've been friends long enough to not stand on formalities at this point in our lives? What is it, Digger?"

"All right, now, I've told you this is weird. So, we've lived on the Keweenaw Peninsula since we were born, and over the years we've both heard a lot of Indian myths and stories, right?"

Rex nods affirmatively. "And, a lot of Finnish tales and ghost stories too. Okay, so?"

"I drove over to Baraga yesterday to offer some yard work to a few guys, and I saw this old Chippewa fella I know prancing around near the tribal center as if he'd won the lottery."

"And!?" Rex prompts.

"And so, I asked him what he was so excited about. He whooped around and said, 'It's true! The prophesy is true!' The old guy, I think his name is Walter, started to prance away, and I asked him what prophesy he was talking about. He looked at me cautiously and whispered, 'The sacred Megis shell is real, and its healing powers are boundless!'"

Rex had a look of skeptical annoyance on his face and replied, "Hell, Digger, we've been hearing bullshit stories like that all of our lives. You know that!"

"I do know that, Rex, but I also know that Chippewa elder had polio as a child and has never been able to walk without assistance. Now he's hopping around like a teenager. I told you it's weird."

Rex stares at Digger quizzically. "Old Walter? You mean that decrepit old Indian in a wheelchair?!"

"Yep! Same man, boss! Just dancing around, a'hooping and a'hollering!"

Rex looks directly into Digger's eyes trying to divine what this information means. He knows his brain cancer will bring him to his knees and kill him before too long. He's truly scared and feels like he's got nothing to lose by checking out this quirky story.

"When you're finished with your mine tour this morning, Digger, come get me. Let's head over to Baraga. I want to see this for myself."

Robert Midew is a very committed man. He serves as president of the Tribal Council of the Keweenaw Bay Indian Community, and he sometimes quips with associates that he feels like he's the president of three thousand presidents. Having said that, Robert enjoys the support of nearly everyone in their community, and there's nothing that happens on reservation land that he's not aware of. And, in recent days there's been a lot happening.

Robert also possesses very special qualities that are difficult to explain, and an aura around him that many would simply dismiss as his unique personal charm, but there's something deeper than that, something that enables him to see into the heart of things and to connect with people … and animals. Speaking of which, he rarely travels anywhere without his constant companion, a noble beast of a creature that he simply calls Grey. To describe Grey is a challenge. Yes, he's definitely a very large grey canine, but when you look into his eyes, instead of his looking away as most dogs would do, Grey looks deeply into yours with an unspoken message that asks, "Are you really ready for this connection?"

Grey has fallen asleep at Robert's feet as the tribal elders sit around the great table in the Tribal Center. They have come together to speak of the sacred Megis shell and whether to share the knowledge of its special healing properties with the rest of the world. Robert is purposefully remaining silent. He wishes to hear what the other elders say first, and to weigh their words.

Tommy Two Feathers addresses the group. "Forever! That's how long we've preserved and protected the sanctity of the Megis shell. We medicine men have learned its ways, and we've tried to faithfully serve our people well. Why now? Why now should we share what is rightfully ours with those who would steal it from us or belittle its powers? When has the Light-Skinned race ever respected our way of life except for when doing so fattens their wallets?"

A few elders around the table echo his sentiments, and Robert listens patiently as their voices rise in alarm. He shares several of their concerns, and he chooses to listen to everyone's words knowing that something this important demands no less.

"Please tell us, Robert," Willow Starr says after Tommy Two Feathers sits down. "Tell us what discussions you've had with people. Tell us what your heart says."

Robert reaches his hand down and lightly pats behind Grey's ears. The great beast exhales a contented breath, and Robert smiles privately.

Robert stands and begins, "I will tell you what I know, what I believe, and I must say that I do not disagree with any of the concerns that Tommy and the others have voiced. I believe that the prophesies of our elders from eons ago ring as true today as they did then. I believe in the healing power of the Megis shell and the values of living a spiritual and healthy life."

Robert pauses briefly to collect his thoughts. He looks into the eyes of each individual seated around the great table. He wants each to know that he's speaking on a personal level. "The prophets warned us that we shall know the future of our people by the face the Light-Skinned race wears. If they come wearing the face of brotherhood, there will come a time of wonderful change for generations to come. In this way two nations may join to create a mighty nation. If, however, they come carrying weapons or colorful words of greed, we shall know the face of death to our way of life. We should not naively trust what we are told by the Light-Skinned race. They must prove to us they're worthy of our brotherhood and our secrets."

He continues, "My friends, the sacred Megis shell is a gift beyond measure. With the knowledge of our Midewin healers, it's healed the helpless among us and given hope to the hopeless." Robert pauses, then begins again. "With such a gift how can we not share its virtues with others? It's a question that we must ask ourselves, yes? Then there is the financial side that must be considered. I think you all know me well enough by now to know that I'm not motivated by money. Still, there could be a path to prosperity from the power of the Megis that could benefit every Chippewa in ways never before dreamed. The ancient elders warned us about false prophets; people who might use similar words as those that I just posed to you. I agree with that warning, but we must weigh all of the pluses and minuses. How we share such a sacred gift, how we secure our noble heritage, and how we protect ourselves from those who would be greedy are thorny issues we must solve."

"You already know I have spoken with a few individuals I respect at the National Park Service office in Calumet. These are people I believe to be honorable, but what their bosses in Washington might think, I do not know. Grey and I have shared just the smallest bit of what the shell is capable of with them. They now know that we have something very special that can transform the quality of life, spiritually and physically. I have posed our concerns to them without yet revealing the full transformative power of the Megis shell. We have agreed to continue our conversations, but I have told them that we Chippewas will not go public unless we feel respected and forever secure. Nothing short of that will work. I promise to keep each of you informed as things unfold to share with our people. That is all I know."

The members of the tribal council sit stone still at the great table considering Robert's words. Each one nods his or her understanding. Several offer respectful words of support to Robert, and then they all recede from the room. Willow remains behind.

"Robert, you and I have known each other for many years. We played together in the woods and along the shores of Gitche Gumee. We went to the reservation's school together. I was here when you returned from your military tours, and each of us has served our tribal community in our own ways. And, we've been intimate. I feel like I know you as well as anyone, and yet there is a nature about you that I don't know at all. It is like your face has a veil that I cannot see through. It's as if Grey is the only creature that fully understands your ways. I say these things not out of concern or envy. I sense you have your secrets and your purpose which are paths that you feel you must walk alone. I want you to know that you can count on our friendship, and I will support whatever decisions you believe are right for our people." She kisses Robert lightly on the cheek and gently touches between Grey's eyes.

"It is indeed a lonely path that I follow, Willow, but it is the only way I know to be true to both our people and the Megis shell. Please don't mistake this as meaning that I don't care for you. You're special to me, a gift from Manitou, but I feel the burden of thousands of years of Anishinaabe and Chippewa teachings, and I must now forego the pleasures of your company and remain focused on the future of our people. Perhaps it will not always be that way. I welcome that day, my dear friend."

Chapter 3

"ARE YOU ALL PACKED UP for your trip to Michigan?" Mace asks me.

"Yeah, pretty much," I reply. "Just a few more things to throw in Pappy, and I'll be ready to hit the road." Pappy is the nickname I've given to my Toyota Tacoma pickup. I've owned it for twenty-plus years now, and it's still running fine. Well, fine ever since I put new tires, shocks, wipers, brakes, and boosted up the freon on the old truck.

Mace and I are standing in our antique camera museum checking out a few recent acquisitions for the collection. The crown jewel is still the daguerreotype camera that once belonged to artist and inventor, Samuel Morse. It's arguably the rarest camera in the world because the inventor of photography, Louis Daguerre, gifted it to Samuel Morse who then used it to introduce photography to America. In addition to my paying a lot of dough for it, it came at an even steeper price because my childhood friend, Weed Rawlins, was gunned down by an assassin during that time. In some ways I view this famous camera as having an indelible stain on it that only my close family of friends and I can see.

"So are you taking the Demon camera with you?" Mace asks.

I look at him and nod my head affirmatively. The Demon camera is a nineteenth-century metal detective camera that fits in the palm of my hand. Years ago Mace and Weed modified several of my antique cameras into killing devices that I used when I was in full, avenging, vigilante mode. I like the Demon in particular because it shoots out a highly charged arc of blue electricity that literally fries anyone who gets in its way. Some people like handguns. Me, I'm a photographer and an antique camera collector, so something like the Demon is more my style. And by the way, I'm not looking for anyone to approve of my using weapons, except maybe Maggie, but being armed and willing to use force to defend myself or others has saved lives. Okay, it's ruined a few too, but those jerks deserved it. So, go get sanctimonious with someone else. Just sayin!

Mace and I take my home elevator upstairs to our main living quarters, and Maggie tells me I had a phone call a few minutes ago.

"Who was it?" I ask, anxious to hit the road.

"Banks!" she replies not knowing whether to be happy to hear from a man who was my compatriot in saving our son, Bodie, and President Jake Horvath from the Russians five years ago, or scared shitless because of the terrifying memories that episode dredges up.

"How'd he sound?" I ask.

"Normal," she says, "but with the kind of scary stuff you guys get involved in, being normal isn't exactly a ringing endorsement."

She's right, of course, but I choose not to engage in that topic any further. She gives me his number up at the Cedar Island lodge on the Brule River in Northern Wisconsin, and I walk out onto the deck to call him back.

"Banks, to what do I owe the pleasure of your call?"

"Hello, Clay, it's great to hear your voice. It's been too long. Maggie told me you're about to hit the road for Michigan, so I won't keep you long, but Jake Horvath has some free time since he's no longer president, and he's coming up to join me for a few days of fly fishing. He asked me if Bodie is up at Camp Voyager again this summer, and if so, he thought it might be fun for the three of us to do some fishing together. Of course, you're perfectly welcome to join us if you're free."

"Well darn, that would be great if I weren't already committed for this photography assignment near Sleeping Bear Dunes, but Bodie would be thrilled. Why don't I call the camp director, Bern Lorber, and let him know it's fine with Maggie and me, and that he can expect a phone call from you soon, okay?"

"Oorah that!" Banks replies. "Maybe you can catch a quick flight up here after your photo shoot and join us."

"Very tempting, but I also promised my other son, Rennie, that I'd drive up and meet him on the Keweenaw Peninsula for a few days. I sure wish I could join you, but I don't think it'll work this time. I'd love for us to do it another time though."

"We'll make sure that happens," Banks says. "So, you're going up to the Keweenaw, huh? Copper country. That's a coincidence! I have an old marine buddy that lives up there. His name's Robert Midew. In fact, Robert was a very important part of our small circle of marines that Jake Horvath and I knew we could stake our lives on. Essentially, it was Jake, our sharpshooter, Chris Helton, Robert Midew, me, and a couple of other guys. We made it through hell and back in Iraq and Afghanistan, but a bunch of our guys weren't so lucky. We survivors all keep in touch though and remember our buddies who didn't make it. If you get into a bind up there, Robert's the man for you to call."

"How do I reach him, if I need to?" I ask.

"He's the president of the Keweenaw tribal council of Chippewa Indians. I'll text his phone number to you.

"Chippewa, huh!" I say. "My son, Rennie, says he may be doing some research on an old Indian artifact as part of his summer internship."

"Well, if it's anything really important, you can count on Robert knowing about it. In fact, he's probably one of the more unusual and mysterious men I've ever known."

"In what way?" I ask Banks.

"He's hard to describe, but beyond a doubt he's the single best warrior I've ever known. It's like he has this sixth sense that tells him when danger is around, and I've never seen anyone attack an enemy with the ferocity that he can bring. He's almost invisible like the wind, and just as swift. Seriously, Clay, if you or Rennie get into a bind, call Robert."

"Thanks, Banks. I will."

We talk a few minutes longer, mostly about trout and the Brule River, and then we hang up. Banks's words about his Chippewa buddy stay with me though. You never know when you can use a friend who moves like the wind.

Thirty minutes later I've made my phone call to Bern Lorber about Bodie fishing with Banks and Jake, and I've said my goodbyes to my lovely Maggie, Tori, Mace, and Satchmo. Finally, I'm ready to hit the road. No matter how much I love being at our home, starting a new adventure on the road is always a thrill. I put Pappy into drive, turn on my favorite Weed Rawlins CD, and head north for Michigan.

The drive is not unfamiliar to me. Over the years I've spent a fair amount of time in Michigan beginning when I was a kid vacationing with my parents in Charlevoix and then with Maggie, Bodie, and Rennie in different places along the Leelanau peninsula. I pretty much know where I'm going, and despite the nuisances of summer highway construction, the solo drive is a welcome change of pace. A couple of hours later Indiana is in Pappy's rearview mirror, and I'm cruising up the western side of Michigan.

I call Tippy McClain who's the director of the visitors bureau in Empire. She's my contact for my photography assignment with the bureau, and she's also made lodging accommodations for me. I'm not exactly sure why she wants me to return for more shots since I thought we had their promotional project satisfactorily completed, but Tippy insisted that we do some night shots as well. And, who am I to argue with a client when it comes to taking pictures of the Milky Way? She answers the phone on the second ring.

"Hi Tippy, it's Clay. Am I catching you at a good time?"

"Hey there, Clay, it's great to hear your voice, and yes, I can talk now. When am I going to see your handsome face up here?"

"A couple of hours yet. I got a little bit of a late start, and right now I'm just north of South Haven. Can you text me the address of where I'm staying. I figure I'll get up to Empire around four o'clock."

"Sure thing, Clay, I booked you a room in a very sweet cottage on Lake Michigan. Lovely view, very private. I'll text you the address, and we can meet there, okay? We can firm up your assignment then."

"Sounds good, Tippy, I look forward to getting your text, and I'll call you again as I get closer to the cottage."

Tippy's a seasoned professional, and my guess is she does a very good job running the visitors bureau. I worked with her just once before, and it was a positive experience. My only caution is that she gets a little too cozy occasionally. I mean, nothing really overt, but in subtle ways I've tried to make it clear that I'm a very happily married guy. I believe she's divorced, and she's an attractive enough middle-aged woman, so I imagine she has her share of suitors. I just don't want to be one of them. It's a curse being such a dashing stud. Okay, I'm just kidding, well mostly.

I continue driving north along the eastern shoreline of Lake Michigan passing through resort towns like Pentwater, Ludington, and Manistee. The weather is clear with some gray haze over the big lake. I check my weather app, and it appears I should have mostly clear days and nights for my photography. I receive Tippy's text with the address for my lodging and call her again about an hour later to let her know I'm getting near.

"Oh good, Clay, you're only about a mile away now. I'll meet you outside to help you unload your gear." Tippy says.

Two minutes later I pull down a tree-lined gravel driveway at the end of which I see a sturdy pine log cottage and the big lake beyond. Tippy is waiting outside pointing to where I should park.

"Hi there!" I say exiting Pappy. "Nice place. Whoever owns it is pretty lucky."

"Thanks!" Tippy says as she gives me a welcoming hug. "It's mine. I picked it up over the winter when the real estate prices were lower."

"Oh, so I'm bunking at your place, right?" I say with a little confusion because she hadn't mentioned anything about staying with her.

"Yeah Clay, I hope that's all right with you. I've got plenty of space. It'll be fun."

"Uh sure," I reply. I mean, it's a really nice looking place from the outside, and the last thing I want to do is be rude to a client. Nonetheless, it's a surprising development which I'll just have to graciously deal with. I collect my gear, and Tippy shows me to the guest room which is down the hall from her bedroom. My room is very nicely decorated, and my immediate thought is that Maggie would really enjoy this place.

"After you get settled, Clay, why don't you meet me on the patio. I've got some beverages and a snack, and we can talk about your shooting locations."

"Sounds good, Tippy, I'll be with you in a few minutes. After we talk I think I want to take a little nap so I can be rested for staying out late shooting the night sky over the sand dunes. I've really been looking forward to doing this ever since you suggested it for your publicity campaign."

"Sounds good, Clay, I'll see you in a couple of minutes then, and maybe I could join you at the dunes. It sounds, uh, very romantic."

I let her last comment slide and retreat into my room to freshen up and charge my cameras' batteries.

"There you are," Tippy chirps as I walk out onto the patio. "Everything to your satisfaction?"

"Yeah, everything's fine. You have a great place, thanks!"

"So, why don't you make yourself comfortable, Clay? Have something to drink and some refreshments, and we can talk about what to photograph."

"You know, honestly Tippy I thought we got everything you wanted last time. I'm happy to do more, but let me know what you're thinking."

"Well, of course you're right, Clay. You did capture several years' worth of great promotional images for the visitors bureau last time. You know I just thought we hit it off so well, and I know you love shooting night sky images, so I just thought it would be fun to accompany you to the dunes under a starry sky."

Okay, so right about now my bullshit meter is in the caution zone because I'm not exactly sure where Tippy is coming from about us being under the stars together.

"Well, of course, you know I'm a happily married man," I say with some levity in case my bullshit meter is out of whack.

Tippy laughs and gives me a steamy look that means she thinks I'm adorable. Oh, swell!

"Well, of course you are, Clay. This is strictly business," she says half-convincingly. "What time should we head out?"

"Well, er, uh," I stammer. "You know, Tippy, I'm used to working alone. It's kind of a monastic experience for me."

"Well, lucky for you I can help tote some stuff like wine and snacks. What time?" Tippy repeats with a tone that says, "Sir, you might as well just give in."

So, I say what any secure, strong-willed professional and married guy would say, "Uh, about eleven o'clock."

"Great! You're on your own for dinner. I'll meet you here at eleven o'clock. Can't wait!" Tippy turns and sashays back inside.

I stand there feeling rather sheepish wondering what the hell that was all about, and if I need to grab my Demon camera in case I have to defend my honor under the stars. I always pack it anyway, but how could I ever use it on someone who thinks I'm adorable. Where's Maggie when I need a strong woman to protect me?

Chapter 4

DIGGER FINN STEERS the Brockway Mining Company's Cadillac Escalade into the parking lot of the Chippewa tribal center in Baraga. He looks over at Rex Trammer in the passenger seat and sees that his boss's eyes are closed. He's not sure if Rex is asleep or privately contemplating his coming demise.

"We're here, boss," he says softly. He points and says, "Over there's where I saw old Walter whooping it up."

Rex opens his eyes and sees that Digger is pointing to the sidewalk by the tribal center. No one is there, but Digger says, "C'mon, let's get out and see who's around."

The two men slide out of their seats and walk to the entrance of the tribal center. Rex stands still for a few moments and closes his eyes again, feeling the warm sunshine's healing energy. When he reopens his eyes he sees Robert Midew standing in front of him.

"Oh, Robert! I didn't hear you come up. You were as quiet as, uh, an Indian." He smiles weakly as he voices his insensitive comment.

"Hello, Rex. It's been a while since I've seen you. I heard that you've been ill. What brings you to our little part of the world?"

"I'm surprised that you know I've been ill. I just found out a few days ago myself."

Robert nods knowingly, "Information has a way of flowing to me."

Neither Rex or Digger knows what that means.

"Do you mind if we come inside, Robert? There's something that Digger shared with me that I'd like to discuss with you."

Robert sweeps his arm in a welcoming motion, and the three of them enter the tribal center's great room. Rex's eyes dart around taking in the Chippewa artifacts lining the large room's walls and in display cases.

"Have you ever been in here before?" Robert asks Rex and Digger. "There's a lot of history displayed here, some good, some not so pleasant."

Rex takes his comment in stride but regards it as a swipe against the Light-Skinned race.

"First time inside here," Rex admits. Digger nods his agreement.

They sit down in the great room, and Robert asks somberly, "How far along is your cancer, Rex?"

"How'd you know that I have cancer, Robert?"

Robert shrugs and repeats himself, "Information has a way of flowing to me."

"My cancer will kill me before too long," Rex replies evenly.

"I'm very sorry for you and your loved ones. I hope that you remain comfortable for as long as possible. Please tell me what it is that brings you men to Baraga today?"

Rex glances over at Digger and nods for him to speak.

"Actually Robert I was here a few days ago, and I ran into old Walter. I was shocked by how youthful and healthy he appeared."

"Ah yes, Walter!" Robert beams. "That old feller is a bit of an enigma, isn't he?"

"I'd say so," Digger replies. "I saw him dancing and prancing around like he was a kid. Any idea how an old guy who had polio got so youthful?"

Robert shrugs dismissively. "Like I said, "Old Walter is a bit of a mystery." Robert stands up and says, "Now, I know you two are very busy men so I won't keep you."

"Please, Mr. Midew, can we please just have a few more minutes of your time?" Rex asks respectfully. Robert retakes his seat, and Rex nods for Digger to speak again.

"When I was here," Digger continues, "Walter whispered to me, 'The Megis shell is real, and that its healing powers are boundless.' I took that as the musings of an old man at first, but seeing him in such good health after spending a lifetime struggling with the effects of polio made me wonder. Any idea what that's about?"

Robert shrugs again. "The world is a mysterious place, yes? Old Walter would be wise not to speak of the Megis shell so freely, especially to those who do not honor its ways."

Digger begins to speak again, but Rex interrupts him. "Robert, I'm a dying man. I've tried to live a good life, and I readily admit that I haven't t always shown as much integrity as I should've, especially to the people of your race, but staring death in the face brings a certain, uh, clarity of thinking … and humility. Please tell me. Is there anything supernatural about your sacred Megis shell? Anything that can help me live a longer and more charitable life?"

Robert listens very closely to Rex's words. He feels sympathy for him as another human being. He knows that Rex is a man asking for a lifeline. He's desperate but not yet totally resigned to his fate.

Robert looks around the room at the various cultural relics on display. He sees ancient deerskin clothing, brightly beaded head bands and headdresses, cradleboards, drums, finely crafted weapons and bows, and old copper implements. He hears the distant voices of Anishinaabe and Chippewa elders, the prophets. The voices remind him about the Light-Skinned race, "Do not accept them in total trust. Make them prove themselves to you."

"I can be helpful to your people, if you give me a chance," Rex adds plaintively.

"A chance, Mr. Trammer. A chance like the one you and the Brockway Mining Company never gave my people, ever! A chance, you say!"

Rex Trammer sees the resolve in Robert's eyes. He knows that he will never know if the sacred Megis shell that old Walter extolled has the power to save him. He nods and begins to stand up when he is suddenly overcome with a debilitating pain in his head. He moans balefully as he reaches up to hold his throbbing forehead. "Aaahhaahh!" And then Rex crashes face first onto the great room's council table.

Digger immediately runs to help his boss, and Robert tells him, "Stay here with him. I'll return in a moment." Robert exits the room as Digger helps settle Rex back into his chair. Rex has a cut above his brow and a small amount of blood oozes from his nose, but he appears to be slowly recovering some composure. His pain is excruciating though.

Robert returns a moment later holding a glowing deerskin pouch and moves next to Rex. "Stand back!" he commands Digger who immediately complies. Robert utters an ancient Chippewa incantation, spreads a few dried herbs on Rex's head and in his mouth, and the glow from something within the bag shoots out and engulfs Rex Trammer's aching, bloody head. Another moment later and the glowing energy force is gone. Rex spits out the remaining herbs, and stands up.

"What the hell did you do, Robert? One moment I have a splitting headache, and I'm sure I'm gonna die, and the next thing I know I'm pain-free and feeling strong. Was that from your Megis shell?"

Digger stares in amazement. "See boss, I told you that thing about old Walter was true."

Robert tells them again, "Remain here. I'll return in a moment."

"Are you okay, boss?" Digger asks with serious concern.

"Yeah, I'm okay now. I never felt anything like that, Digger. Never! Whatever Robert has, it's made me feel better than I have for a long, long time. We've got to get our hands on that thing, Digger."

Robert returns and sees his two visitors huddled together.

"I don't know what the hell you did to me, Mr. Midew, but I'll make it worth your while to give me access to it whatever it is. Hell, I'll give you $1 million for it … today!"

Robert looks at him and shakes his head. "You come to our tribal place and dare to insult us with money. You think you can buy anything, including longer life. You insult yourself by even asking me."

"Damnit, I'll give you $10 million, Mr. Midew. You can have it tomorrow. That's a lot of money for your people. You can improve your schools, have a regular doctor, hell you can keep it all for yourself for all I care!"

"I'm glad you're feeling better, Mr. Trammer. That will only be temporary. The discomfort will recur with even greater intensity and duration. I suggest you seek medical attention for pain. Don't return here and never again insult me and our people with your pitiful bribery. Your visit is over. Now leave!"

The two men see that Robert Midew is resolute in his banishment of them. They get up from the table and slowly exit the tribal center. As they get into the Cadillac they see old Walter spryly ambling down the sidewalk. He gives them a hearty wave and walks around a corner.

"Digger, this isn't over," Rex forecasts. "I can't believe how good that thing made me feel. If I can get my hands on that Megis shell, it could be the answer to my prayers. Without it, I'm screwed. We need to think, Digger. We need to figure out how to get that shell and snatch someone, other than Robert, who knows how to use it. Or, maybe grab someone that Robert cares about and is willing to trade for it."

Chapter 5

GO OUTSIDE TO PAPPY a few minutes before eleven to stow my camera gear. I've done this so often that I know where I want each item positioned. Most nights that I photograph the night sky I like using my Canon 5D Mark IV camera with a variety of Canon and Rokinon wide-angle lenses. I always keep extra batteries charged and have my intervalometer handy for long exposures to capture star trails.

I'm ready to head out, and at precisely eleven o'clock Tippy arrives looking fresh and buoyant carrying a wicker basket, no doubt concealing goodies and who knows what else.

"Hey Clay, lovely night! Are you ready to head out on our little adventure?"

"Yep," I chirp. Truth is, I've been really looking forward to shooting the night sky over Sleeping Bear Dunes for a long time. When I was a much younger guy getting started with photography, I studied the work of the greats like Edward Weston, Ansel Adams, and Edward Curtis. The way they captured sand dunes and grassy landscapes fascinates me to this day. So now I want to do similar images, except at night. I'm not thrilled about having Tippy along for the ride because I'm serious about my work, and she's becoming a bit of a distraction. I'm gonna stay focused and positive and get the shots that I came for. Right?

We get Tippy's basket stowed away and climb into Pappy. "How old is this truck, Clay? Shouldn't it be in a museum or a used car lot or something?" she teases.

"Pappy's going to be twenty-one in November. I bought him new, and he's been a great ride ever since. Maggie keeps wanting me to get something else, but I think Pappy still has some good years left."

"Well, I'm happy for you and Pappy!" she laughs.

I steer the Tacoma onto M-22 North and a few miles later Tippy tells me to turn. "There's a great secluded point up ahead that very few people know about, Clay. Slow down a little so we don't miss the turn off."

Soon enough we see an unmarked sandy road leading toward the crest of a sand dune high above Lake Michigan. We drive down the deserted road, and I pull Pappy over to an area that seems to have solid ground underneath it. I kill the headlights, and we step out to the silence of nighttime under a brilliant star-studded sky. It's mesmerizing in its beauty and humbling in its infiniteness.

"Wow!" is about the only word I can immediately muster. I see an old observation platform that'll provide solid footing for my tripod, and I begin unloading my gear and walk over to the platform. Instinctually, I look south this time of year knowing that the dramatic galactic center of the Milky Way will be in full view during the time we're here. Tippy pulls out her wicker basket, two sling chairs, and a blanket and joins me near the platform.

As far as I'm concerned I'm here on a photographic assignment and Tippy can entertain herself however she wants. A couple of minutes later I hear a pop and know that she's selected wine as her first choice of entertainment.

I position my tripod so that the Lake Michigan shoreline forms an arcing panorama with the Milky Way stretching down to meet it. I keep my white balance set at 5000 Kelvin for natural colors and begin taking twenty-five-second exposures.

"I'm liking what I see, Tippy." By now our eyes have adjusted to the darkness, and I use my green laser pointer to show Tippy where Jupiter is and Saturn and Antares as well. I take another twenty-five-second exposure adjusting my camera's white balance to 3200 giving the scene a much bluer tone that some people find appealing.

About fifteen minutes later Tippy sidles alongside me and asks, "Can I take a look, Clay?"

"Okay, but please don't touch the tripod or the camera otherwise I'll have to refocus."

I smell the wine on Tippy's breath and hear her giggle as she grabs hold of my arm to steady herself. I show her the last shot I took on the view screen, and she shows her enthusiasm by grabbing my arm even more firmly and holding it against her breasts. This arrangement definitely isn't something I had in mind tonight, and I'm trying to do my level best to complete my assignment and not have to babysit an inebriated client.

"Wow, Clay, you're really good at this, aren't you?" Tippy slurs.

Trying not to sound too parental, I ask her, "How much wine have you had?"

"Oh, about half a bottle, maybe more, but don't worry, Clay honey, I've got another bottle for us."

"Oh great," I mumble under my breath as I point my camera in an easterly direction toward Glen Lake. My goal is to capture diagonal star trails over the lake. I was thinking of setting my camera up for a two-hour exposure, but with Tippy being in her cups, I'm not sure if we'll be able to stay out that long. Frankly, I'm beginning to hope that she just falls asleep.

No such luck, Tippy waddles over to her chair and returns carrying a half-consumed wine bottle. "Here you go, Clay!" she laughs as she uses my tripod to steady herself. "Oops! I touched the tripod, didn't I?!" she blurts out. "Here, have some wine."

I'm trying to maintain my patience and suggest that she go sit down so I can work. She puffs out her lower lip and pouts, "Aw c'mon, Clay, it's so pretty out here, and you smell really good."

I turn to face her and remind her that I'm a happily married guy when she plants a big wet kiss on my mouth and massages my butt at the same time.

"All right, Tippy, you're done here," I say with no equivocation in my voice. "You can either go sit down and behave yourself or I'm taking you home. Your choice."

She tries to kiss me again, and I turn away. "Go sit down!" I command. "I'm collecting my gear and we're going back."

"Aw c'mon, Clay, I thought we were having fun."

"Well, I'm not, and you're embarrassing your-self. I think I have all of the pictures I need for one night. We're heading back, Tippy!"

"But, Clay …" she whines as she puts her arms around me. "It's early yet, and no one's around."

I break free, grab my camera and tripod, and head for Pappy. "Let me know if you need help with the chairs and basket," I say over my shoulder. I stow my gear and hear her rattle the chairs as she tosses them in the truck's bed. I help her into the passenger's seat and buckle her seatbelt for her. She's pouting and giggling at the same time.

Thank goodness it's only a few miles back to her cottage, and we drive back in relative silence, with the exception of a couple of aromatic belches coming from my client.

We turn into her driveway, and I see a bright red Dodge Charger parked by her house with a lone figure standing next to it. I hear Tippy say, "Oh shit! It's Maurice."

"So, who's Maurice?" I ask, "And, isn't it a little late for a social visit?"

"Maurice is a guy I've been with a couple of times. I swear, Clay, you sleep with these guys, and they expect you to date 'em afterward. He's usually okay, but he can be a little volatile."

"Oh swell," I say.

I park my car where I did before and exit my truck.

"Who the fuck are you?" Maurice barks menacingly at me, "And what are you doing with my girl?"

"My name's Clay Arnold, and Tippy hired me for a photographic assignment." I try to keep my voice as even as possible, but I'm not liking where I see this encounter heading. Tippy gets out of my truck and staggers a little. "Hi Maurice, what's the good word?" she chirps at the large, lumbering man blocking our way to the cottage.

"Where you been and what're you doing with this dweeb?" he challenges.

"You don't own me, Maurice. Now go home and don't come back until you learn to behave yourself."

Apparently, Maurice didn't appreciate being lectured by "his woman," and he grabs her arm. Tippy winces in pain.

"Okay, sir, that's enough drama. Let her go and dial it down a notch, okay?"

He takes a swing at me and manages to connect with my shoulder. I stumble a little and recover and pull out my phone. "I'm calling 911 so I suggest you crawl back into your vehicle and go cool off somewhere other than here."

"Go home, Maurice!" Tippy slurs at him. "He's just a photographer I hired."

"Did you screw him, Tippy?" he challenges. "Did you?!"

"Maybe I did, and maybe I didn't," she replies adolescently.

He lets go of her arm and turns in my direction. "She's mine!"

"Great!" I say sarcastically, "I'm very happy for both of you. Now, I'm going to bed."

Good ol' Maurice isn't finished proving he's the alpha male though, and he throws another punch at me to prove it. This one connects with my jaw and sends me reeling to the ground. Tippy rushes to help me, and that only pisses off Maurice more.

"Get away from him, Tippy," the big lout snarls.

I stagger to my feet not feeling the least bit pleased with Tippy and her choice of companions. "Look Mr. Maurice," I say. "She's all yours. I've had enough fun with a drunk client and her wacko boyfriend for one night."

That remark pisses him off even more, and he starts coming at me again. I reach my hand inside my pocket and feel a familiar shape. I pull out my Demon camera and quickly place the camera's setting on stun.

"Just stay where you are, will ya? I'm heading inside," I say to the big guy. I look over at Tippy and shake my head in disappointment. She just shrugs sheepishly.

"You're not going inside her house while I'm here, dweeb!" and he lunges at me again but misses.

"Last chance," I say to him, but he lunges awkwardly at me a final time. I press the discharge button on the Demon camera, and a blue arc of electricity shoots out engulfing Tippy's lover boy. He shakes and shimmies for a few long seconds and then drops to the ground. "And, that's what you get for calling me a dweeb!" I say all brave-like.

"Maurice! Honey, are you okay?" Tippy bleats.

"He'll be fine in a few minutes, Tippy, but I'm out of here!" I go inside to my guest room, grab my belongings, trot to my truck, and toss my gear inside Pappy. "This has been swell!" I sarcastically shout to Tippy as I climb inside the safety of my truck and start the engine.

Tippy comes up to my closed window, puckers a kiss, and mouths the words, "Call me!"

I look at her incredulously and pull away wondering where I can find a place to sleep at this hour, and what the hell to tell Maggie, if anything. What a night!

Chapter 6

Rennie walks into the National Park Service office in Calumet to begin his workday and finds his supervisor, Ranger Kelli Katterman, in her office peering intently at a report she just received. Kelli is the education ranger for the Keweenaw National Historic Site, and as such, she's the staff person responsible for presenting and interpreting various cultural sites and artifacts to the public

that are emblematic of the Keweenaw Peninsula's diverse history.

"Hey there Kelli, you're here early as usual," Rennie says to his summer boss. "Looks like you're pretty engrossed in something. Anything I can help you with?"

"Oh hi, Rennie, I didn't hear you come in. Yeah, well maybe, actually I'm not exactly sure. I think I was accidentally copied on a communique between our local director and the national office in Washington. In your studies, Rennie, have you ever come across something called a Megis shell? It's also called a Cowrie shell. The Chippewa revere the Megis shell as something sacred and mystical."

"Naw, I'm from Indiana, and we don't have a lot of shells. I don't think I'm familiar with either of those names."

"Honestly, I wasn't either until I came to work on the Keweenaw a couple of years ago, but as I spent time on the reservation and at the tribal center, I learned much more about their Chippewa culture. The president of the local Indian community is a very interesting man named Robert Midew. He actually has a really big wolf as his steady companion. Robert is full-blooded Chippewa, and he's made certain that as the park service's education ranger, I've been exposed to as much of their culture as possible. It's very important to him that I accurately teach the tribe's ways to the outside community. There's a lot of mythology surrounding the Megis shell because it supposedly has such supernatural healing powers, but I always viewed the stories as a bunch of colorful folklore. From the report I just read, however, it appears that the Megis shell is getting a ton of attention from Washington."

"Very cool!" Rennie says. "Where's the shell now, and how did a seashell find its way up here to the Upper Peninsula of Michigan?"

"Very good questions, Rennie. It appears that the Chippewa tribe has it safely stashed away somewhere. I remember Robert telling me once that many centuries ago his people lived near a great salt water, which he believes was around Maine and the Canadian maritime provinces. It's a known fact that the Chippewa began a great migration that took over five hundred years to complete and eventually led them here to the Upper Peninsula of Michigan and across northern Wisconsin and Minnesota. Robert is pretty tight-lipped when the subject of the Megis shell comes up though. That's why I'm surprised there's any discussion going on between his people and the park service."

"Fascinating and a little spooky too," Rennie says. "So, do you think the Chippewa will share the secrets of the Megis shell?"

"We should know pretty soon, but if white folks treat the Indians the way we have in the past, I doubt the Chippewas will be forthcoming, and frankly I wouldn't blame them."

"Believe me, Kelli, as a person of color, I get it! So, what's on our schedule today?"

"You know, Rennie, I remember that Robert Midew once shared with me that the Megis shell was kept for many years in a very secret sanctuary somewhere on Brockway Mountain. He said that the Midewin, the healers of the Grand Medicine Society, protected the shell and learned the power of its ways. Brockway Mountain is only about thirty miles away, and I was thinking that you and I might take a drive out there and see if we can talk with some of the older locals and maybe the owner of the old Brockway Mining Company. Hopefully, someone can shed some light on this mysterious shell. Are you up for a little road trip with me? It's actually a very pretty drive."

"Sure thing, Kelli! Plus, I imagine I'll be able to use what we learn as additional background material for my doctoral thesis. I'm ready to go whenever you are."

"Great, I'll just sign out and let the staff know where we're going. I also need to make a quick phone call. Why don't I meet you at my car in, say, about fifteen minutes then, okay?"

Eighteen minutes later they exit the parking lot at the Keweenaw Historic Park in Kelli's Subaru Forester and head east on U.S. Route 41 toward Copper Harbor and Brockway Mountain. It's a glorious day to be on the road. The sun is shining warmly. The deciduous trees have leafed out fully. No signs of snow anywhere. And, two enthusiastic young people are cruising around exploring and looking for answers.

"So, Route 41 runs along the spine of the Keweenaw Peninsula, and that's where the majority of the productive copper mines were back in the day," Kelli says. "At one time there were a hundred thousand miners living on the peninsula, mostly immigrants from Finland but many from a lot of other countries as well. It was a very hard life. Miners worked deep underground for long shifts under dirty, dangerous conditions for meager pay. The poor conditions eventually led to bitter labor strikes, and over time the labor issues and the depletion of copper ore caused many mines to close. The communities that had sprung up around the mines eventually withered and died. Today, the remnants of those ghost towns are so meager that no self-respecting ghost would even want to stay there."

"Whew, that's pretty amazing. It's surprising that people put up with such a difficult lifestyle. I had a bit of a rough start myself as a kid, before I met

Clay, my dad, but I never worked underground or had three hundred inches of snow dumped on me."

"Yeah, it's an indication of how difficult things were for a lot of people back in their old country that they chose to immigrate here, plus there was the allure of the American Dream that they'd heard about."

"So, what's our plan? Just drive around until we see someone who we think might know about this mystical, mysterious Megis shell?"

"Well, not exactly," Kelli replies. "Remember I made a call before we left. I have an older mentor who lives on Brockway Mountain just above Copper Harbor. His name's Thomas Arrowsmith, and if anyone living around the mountain knows something, Thomas is the man. He was just retiring from the National Park Service as I was coming on staff as the education ranger. We probably worked together no more than four months, but I learned to be a good listener with Thomas. Toward his last weeks of work, he shared a lot of local lore with me, and I could tell that he believed much of it. Thomas's father was white, and his mother was a full-blooded Chippewa. I shouldn't say was. If I'm not mistaken, she's still alive. She must be close to a hundred years old by now. Thomas told me once that the tribe has medicine men with very special healing powers, and he credited them with her longevity. I just regarded his comment as his feeling proud of his heritage rather than it being exactly true. Now, with all of this speculative talk about the Megis shell, it makes me wonder if there's not a grain of truth to it. Anyway, Thomas has agreed to see us, but I have a feeling he's going to be somewhat reluctant to say much about the shell. I guess we'll see."

With light traffic Kelli's Forester cruises along the highway zipping past the ghost towns of Mohawk, Central, Delaware, and Mandan. From Mandan the scenery takes on a different look, going from open land to mature forests of birches, maples, poplars, and pines forming a verdant canopy over the road. Somehow, the scene looks different, normal-looking, and yet richer and alive.

"So, Rennie, you mentioned that you had a rough start in life. Do you mind sharing what that was like?"

"No, I don't mind. It's not something I think much about because, well, it was pretty unpleasant, and my life is really good now. So, I prefer to think about the positive rather than dwell on the negative. Essentially, I was like a street rat living by myself in an abandoned shack in Indianapolis. I didn't go to school, and I learned how to avoid the cops and school authorities. I'd probably be dead today if it weren't for Clay and Mace plucking me up and taking me to their home."

"Why did they do that?" Kelli asks in confusion.

Rennie laughs ironically and says, "It's a pretty amazing story when you think about it, and I still shake my head in how lucky I was. When I was really little, like five or six, Clay had come to the south side of Indy taking photographs for an exhibit about inner-city street life. He took a picture of me sitting in the shadowed doorway of an old tenement building. The image received international acclaim. We still have the picture. I've saved it on my phone, and I'll show it to you later. Anyway, apparently Clay was really struck with empathy when he saw me, and the image wouldn't leave him. So, he and Mace came looking for me. They found me living alone in squalor, and offered me work and a place to live. I reluctantly agreed. The first couple of weeks were a little rocky, but once I realized that Clay, Mace, Tori, and Weed who's now dead, were good people I could trust, well, things got easier, and before long I became part of the family. That was a different lifetime ago, one that I don't dwell on, but one that I don't ever want to forget either. Clay and Mace literally saved me, and Maggie and Tori made sure I had a really good education and helped guide me to where I am today."

"That's an incredible story," Kelli says. "I can't even imagine what it must've been like for you in the beginning. Your family has been so supportive of you."

"Yeah, it's pretty incredible," Rennie says softly. "And, I think that because of my early years as a black kid, I became interested in sociology, and how different races interact the way they do."

"So, why did you choose the Keweenaw Peninsula for your doctoral internship. It's pretty remote here."

"Yeah, it's definitely remote, but that's part of the allure for me. It's a fascinating field of study since you have the confluence of Native Americans and people with ancestries from all over Europe, Africa, South America, and even the Middle East. A lot has already been studied and written about the struggle of African Americans, but I learned that not enough had been researched about the races that settled in Copper Country. So, that's why I decided to come up here."

Kelli looks over at Rennie with increased respect and smiles warmly at him. "Well, Rennie Cotton, I'm really glad you did, and I hope your summer with us will be memorable."

"Thanks, Kelli, me too. It's sure been interesting so far."

As they pass Lake Medora, Rennie's phone rings, and he sees that it's Clay calling him. He answers the phone. "Hey Dad, I'm on the road right now with Ranger Kelli. We're heading to Brockway Mountain. How's it going?"

"Hi son, I wanted you to know that my photography assignment at Sleeping Bear Dunes ended early, and I'm on the road to Calumet. I just crossed over the Mackinac Bridge, and I should be up there in a few hours."

"Wow, great! I'm not sure how long Kelli and I will be on the mountain, but you've got my apartment's address, and I left a spare key under the doormat. If you get there before I get back, just let yourself in. There's food in the fridge and pantry so just make yourself comfortable, okay? I shouldn't get home too late."

"Sounds good, Rennie. Please tell Kelli that I look forward to meeting her. Has there been any more progress in deciding if the Chippewa artifact you mentioned is going to be made available to the public?"

"Not yet, Dad, but Kelli thinks we should know more pretty soon. We're actually going to see one of her mentors for more background information. It's kinda mysterious. Really no telling where this will lead, so I hope you don't mind staying a little flexible."

"Will do. So, I'll see you in a few hours, son. Be safe, okay?" I hang up with Rennie and begin driving west across the Upper Peninsula of Michigan.

"I'm really looking forward to meeting your dad, Rennie. I still can't believe that the famous Clay Arnold is coming up to our little part of the world."

"He's just a regular guy, Kelli. I think the two of you will get along great."

Before long they see signs for Copper Harbor, and Kelli takes the turn for the Brockway Mountain Road. "Thomas said to keep our eyes peeled for a wooden sign by his mailbox. He said it's got an engraving of a horizontal arrow with the name Smith under it … Arrowsmith."

A few minutes later Rennie sings out, "There it is!" They turn down the retired ranger's gravel driveway and see a fit-looking man with neatly cropped gray hair splitting firewood. Behind him they see his tidy log cabin nestled in the trees and a panoramic view of Lake Superior.

Kelli pulls her Forester over to an area where her mentor is pointing, and they get out.

"You made it!" Thomas Arrowsmith calls out to them as he wipes the sweat from his brow with a red handkerchief. "Welcome!"

"Hey Thomas, great to see you!" Kelli says as she gives her old colleague a friendly hug. "So, this is how a retired ranger spends his time, huh? Surrounded by nature with no one around. You've got a great place."

"Thanks, Kelli, it looks like your work with the park service agrees with you, and who is this fine gentleman you brought along?"

"This fine gentleman is Mister Rennie Cotton from a faraway place called Indiana. Rennie's doing a summer internship with us as part of his doctoral work in sociology at Northwestern."

"Hmmm, sounds very impressive. Can he speak?" Thomas teases with a twinkle in his eye.

"Hello, Mr. Arrowsmith. It's a pleasure to meet you, sir!"

"Oh, and he's polite and well-spoken too. Welcome to my home, Rennie. Any friend of Kelli's is a friend of mine. Why don't you two come inside, and we can get something to drink and talk a bit."

They walk inside Thomas's cabin and see an interior that is well-kept with old photographs and paintings thoughtfully placed on the walls and Keweenaw artifacts occupying various niches. It looks like a very personal collection of objects, some that are Chippewa, others that are representative of the white Europeans who settled in the region, while several others that display colorful rocks and copper, animal skulls, and dried leaves and herbs.

"Wow, Mr. Arrowsmith, given the diversity of your collection, I bet I could learn a lot for my doctoral thesis. I'd love my dad to see what you've collected."

"Thanks, Rennie, what you see is a lifetime of acquiring different things that resonate with me. Is your dad a collector too?"

"Yeah, but Dad collects antique cameras and early optical devices."

"Rennie's father is Clay Arnold, the photographer," Kelli adds.

"Really?" Thomas says. "Everyone knows the name, Clay Arnold, and for very good reason. I know he's had a long and illustrious career. I recall seeing several of his night sky photographs that were spellbinding."

"Yeah, that's my dad," Rennie says as he puffs his chest out with pride. He's on his way up here to meet me, and I know he'd love to see your collection and meet you."

"Well, maybe we can make that happen," Thomas replies. "Besides seeing you, what else brings Clay Arnold up to the Keweenaw Peninsula?"

"Well honestly, when I heard that the Chippewas might unveil a special artifact, I got all excited and told Kelli and her supervisor that my dad might be willing to photograph the tribe's presentation. I got a little ahead of myself because I hadn't discussed it with Dad, but he said he'd be willing to do it if folks were interested. I guess I was trying to impress people and shouldn't have done that, but Dad says he'd be happy to help."

Thomas turns to Kelli and says, "I see that your friend, Rennie Cotton, has a good heart. Nothing wrong with showing some enthusiasm. As I recall, there was an eager young ranger named Kelli Katterman not too long ago who showed a similar amount of enterprising spirit, eh, Kelli?"

Kelli blushes with the truth.

Thomas pours three glasses of lemonade and places cookies and fruit on a plate. "C'mon, let's sit by the picture window and talk about what you're looking for."

From his large picture window they can see a vast sea of deep green pines that nicely frame a view of Copper Harbor and its lighthouse. And beyond that, the steel gray expanse of Gitche Gumee, Lake Superior. It's a view one could never grow weary seeing. It has a calming, centering effect just looking out the window.

"Wow! That's quite a view!" Rennie says.

"You ought to see it in winter," Thomas replies. "It's magical!"

Once they sit down Kelli begins, "Thomas, it's awfully good of you to let Rennie and me invade your piece of paradise here. There's quite a buzz going on at the National Park Service about this supposedly sacred Megis shell that Robert Midew and the Chippewa tribe say has very special powers that they might be willing to share. Robert mentioned to me once that the Megis had been safely hidden in a shrine of some sort on Brockway Mountain. On our own, Rennie and I thought it would be interesting to speak with some of the locals around the mountain to see what information we could learn. Naturally, given your background and knowledge, I thought of you. Can you tell us what you know?"

"Perhaps," Thomas Arrowsmith answers evasively. "But, first you need to understand that there is no 'supposedly' when it comes to the Megis shell being sacred and having mystical powers. Those who know its ways and accept them find an inner well-being that is beyond description. I was skeptical for a long time. In fact, I never spoke of it because I didn't want to embarrass myself talking about some magic gastropod. Over time, however, especially as I saw the healing impact it had on my mother, I began to believe in the shell's power."

"Really?!" Kelli replies. "You honestly believe that there's something to this story?"

"I do, Kelli, and quite a few other people do to, mainly Chippewas, of course, but over time the Midewin healers have unlocked many of the shell's mysteries. I've never seen it, but I have seen the results of its power."

Rennie and Kelli sit stone still listening as Thomas recounts a few episodes in which the Megis shell was responsible for inexplicable healings.

"And then, of course, there's my mother who will turn one hundred soon, and old Walter at the reservation near Baraga. He had polio as a boy and could never walk without assistance. Now, I hear he's strutting around like a young rooster. Some say all because of the Megis shell."

"Do you know where the sacred shrine was hidden on the mountain?" Rennie asks.

"Yes and no," comes Thomas's confusing reply. "I just know that it was hidden deep underground on Brockway Mountain not far from the mining company that bears its name, but I never heard precisely where."

"Do you think Rennie and I are crazy coming out here looking for answers?"

Thomas exhales a hearty laugh. "Crazy? No, I would never think that about you, Kelli. A little young and naive perhaps but why not look around and ask questions? I once asked Robert about the shell's location, and despite our long association, he would never commit to telling me where the shell is or what it's precisely capable of doing. That's another reason why I came around to believing in the power of the sacred shell. I figured if Robert wouldn't tell me, there must be an extremely good reason for his secrecy."

"So who else do you suggest that we talk to?" Rennie asks. "Should we speak with the owner of the Brockway mine?"

Thomas visibly winces a little at that suggestion. "Rex Trammer is a wealthy and powerful man, but he's never been a good friend to the Chippewa people. For years I tried to get him to hire folks from the reservation, and to also be more charitable with their needs. He wasn't even mildly interested. You could try to talk with him, but I doubt that he would know very much, if anything. I'd be shocked if Robert and the Chippewas would be willing to tell him anything significant. Having said that, you never know what someone knows until you ask them, right?"

"Would you be willing to call Mr. Trammer to see if he'd be amenable to letting Rennie and me visit him while we're out here?"

Thomas didn't hesitate with his reply. "No, I wouldn't, Kelli. Rex and I have never been close, partly because he was a big CEO, and I was some lowly half-breed guy working for the National Park Service. No, I'm afraid he wouldn't even take my call. But heck, no reason why you shouldn't give it a try. The Brockway Mining Company is only a fifteen minute drive from here, and sometimes cold calls are the best way to get results."

The three of them chatted for another ten minutes or so, and then Thomas said he needed to get back to his chores. "Great seeing you, Kelli, and thanks for looking me up. We old retired guys like company every once in a while. I wish you good luck with Rex Trammer, but don't expect a lot from him. And you, Mr. Rennie Cotton, it's been a pleasure meeting you. You're working with a fine woman here and a great professional. I hope our paths cross again before your summer internship is over."

"Thanks, Thomas, I really hope so too!"

Rennie and Kelli say their final goodbyes and climb back into Kelli's Forester. As they slowly pull away, she briefly looks in her rearview mirror and sees Thomas staring at the vast expanse of Lake Superior. Kelli approaches a bend in his driveway and looks a final time in her mirror. She sees a very large grey wolf emerge from the woods that watches them pull away. She starts to say something to Rennie but privately shakes her head in surprise and chooses to keep it as one more mystery of Brockway Mountain.

Chapter 7

R ex Trammer and Digger Finn stand side by side looking out Rex's office window from atop the Brockway Mining Company's number two shaft building. His office is some seventy feet above the ground and provides a broad view of his sprawling property.

"I swear, Digger, I still can't believe how that Megis thing or whatever the hell Robert had in that

pouch made me feel. I was immediately pain free and actually feeling youthful. Damndest thing!"

"I wouldn't have believed it if I hadn't seen it with my own eyes, boss! Question now is how the hell we can get our hands on that thing. Robert implied its healing effects would eventually wear off."

"Yeah, they already are. I feel my energy starting to ebb like a battery losing its juice. Trouble is we don't know where Robert's got that thing stashed. I'm not against just breaking into the place and trashing the joint until we find it, but I'm sure he already knows we might be thinking about that. Robert's smart. He's not going to leave a sacred relic lying around for anyone to swipe it."

"Yeah, you're right, but that may be our only recourse, Rex. He sure made it pretty clear that he wasn't interested in selling it to you. We might just have to bust into the tribal center and take our chances."

"Maybe," Rex voices softly. "Unless we can come up with a better plan, but for the life of me I don't know what." Rex turns away from the window and retreats back to his desk. The pain is increasing in his head, and he prays that it doesn't debilitate him like it did at the tribal center. He knows it's just a matter of time though.

From his vantage point at the window, Digger spies an unfamiliar car pull into their parking lot near the gift shop. Two figures get out.

"We've got company, Rex," he says to his forlorn boss.

"Oh, do you have a mine tour scheduled today?" Rex asks softly.

"No, not this morning. It looks like a female park service ranger and a young black man. I better go down and see what they want."

Rex nods his agreement and stares vacantly at the papers strewn on his desk. A stabbing pain strikes him behind his left eye, and he reaches for another pain pill. Digger looks sadly at the man who was once a captain of industry and exits his office. He takes the elevator down to ground level wondering how much longer his boss will be capable of making decisions.

"Help you folks?" Digger asks Kelli and Rennie as they view the rusty old equipment lying around the mine's grounds.

"Uh, hi, yeah," Kelli says in response as Digger approaches them.

"I'm Kelli Katterman. I'm the education ranger for the National Park Service, and this is my intern, Rennie Cotton. We were hoping to speak with Mr. Trammer if he's available."

"Uh huh," Digger replies. "Well, Mr. Trammer isn't feeling well today. Maybe I can help you?"

"Oh, I'm sorry to hear that. I hope he's feeling better soon. I know this will sound crazy, but Rennie and I drove out from Calumet to see what we could learn about an ancient Indian shrine that we were told is supposedly located somewhere on Brockway Mountain. We just visited with Thomas Arrowsmith who was my mentor at the park service before he retired a little while ago. Thomas seems to think that Mr. Trammer might know something since he and his family have a lot of knowledge about the mountain because of their mining operations."

"Well, miss, I'm not sure how much help we can be. Sure, we've heard stories over the years about Chippewas considering Brockway Mountain to be sacred and all, but we never stumbled upon any shrine."

Just then Rex's voice calls out from behind them. "I see we have visitors from the park service, Digger."

"Jeez boss, I didn't know you were there. This is Kelli. I'm sorry I forgot your last name, miss."

"It's Katterman, Mr. Trammer. I'm Kelli Katterman, the education ranger with the park service, and this is my summer intern, Rennie Cotton."

Rennie nods respectfully, but no handshakes are exchanged.

"Seems like I overheard you mention something about an old Indian shrine and Thomas Arrowsmith."

"That's right," Kelli replies. "Rennie and I just left Thomas, and he thought you might have some information you'd be willing to share."

"Huh, is that right?" Rex returns. "I never knew Ranger Arrowsmith very well. I always dealt with his boss whenever I came into contact with the park service. I understand he's a good man."

"Well, he's certainly been good to me, and I know he's had a very positive reputation within the community. Thomas seems to think you might be willing to speak with Rennie and me."

"Huh, is that so?" Rex says evasively.

There's an awkward pause in the conversation, and Kelli says, "Robert Midew from the Chippewa tribal council has been very helpful to me as well."

That got Rex and Digger's attention, and they each shot a quick sideways glance at the other.

"Oh, so you know Robert, do you? Digger and I visited with him a little bit ago. How well do you know Robert?"

"Actually, I can't say that I know him very well at all," Kelli says, "but he made it clear when I began supervising the park service's education programs that he wanted me to know a lot about the Chippewa's culture and customs so I'd be able to share them accurately with our visitors and students."

"Hmm, is that so?" Rex says. "So, did you and Robert spend much time together?"

"We did, especially in the beginning. Probably a couple of hours each week for the first six months. Now, not so much, but yeah, we keep in touch. He told me once that I'm about the only white person his wolf companion, Grey, is comfortable with, and if you've ever seen Grey, that's a good thing!"

"Yeah, we've seen Grey. Haven't we Digger?"

"Biggest darn canine I've ever seen. That's for sure."

"So, if you're feeling up to it, Rennie and I would like to speak with you a bit about an ancient Chippewa shrine and a special artifact that's created quite a buzz at the park service and our national office."

"Huh, is that so?" Rex says. "A special artifact, huh?! Why don't we go inside. I'd like to hear more about what you're looking for and your relationship with Robert Midew."

"That would be great, Mr. Trammer," Kelli says appreciatively. "I know that Rennie and I should've called you for an appointment, but we didn't know that we should visit with you before Thomas suggested it."

Rex visibly winces as another stab of pain strikes him behind his eyes. "Are you okay, boss?" Digger asks quickly. A moment later Rex says, "I'll be okay. Just give me a second."

Rennie looks at Kelli with concern, and Kelli says, "Mr. Trammer, we can always come back another time if you're not feeling up to this."

"Naw, I'm okay. Let's step inside the shaft building and see what we can learn from each other about this shrine and this artifact that you say everyone's excited about."

The four of them walk inside, and Rennie sees equipment that he never knew existed. Digger says, "This here's a people mover. It goes deep into the mine. One side carried miners, and the other side lifted copper ore from below."

"Wow!" Rennie exhaled. "How deep does the mine go?"

"Over nine thousand feet on an angle, and over six thousand feet straight down. There's ninety-two different levels in the mine, but everything below level seven is flooded."

"Over a mile underground!?!" Rennie blurts out in surprise.

"Yeah," Digger says. "Definitely not someplace you want to be if you don't know your way around, or hell, even if you do," he laughs creepily. "We give mine tours but only on level seven."

The four of them talk for the next twenty minutes, and Kelli shares that the park service has been all atwitter about this sacred artifact called the Megis shell that the park service and the Chippewa community are in negotiations about.

"So, Rennie and I are hoping to see if you and others can shed some light on some special shrine on Brockway Mountain where this Megis shell is supposedly kept."

"Wasn't Robert Midew able to answer your questions?" Rex asks hopefully.

"Well, the sacred shell was about the only think Robert wasn't very forthcoming about. Thomas told me he had a similar experience with Robert, and the two of them have known each other for years."

"Huh, is that so?" Rex says. "Ranger Katterman, would you mind giving Digger and me a few minutes alone. There are some important things I need to discuss with him. You can wait here, and we'll be back very shortly, but something's come up that I need to tell him about."

"Uh sure," Kelli replies. "We've signed out of the office for the entire day, so we can wait a little."

Rex leads Digger to a small makeshift office near the mineshaft's entrance and closes the door.

"What are you thinking, boss?" Digger asks. "Do you honestly think this young ranger and this black fella can help us get the Megis shell? She doesn't seem to know a whole lot."

"Well, I think you're right, Digger. She really doesn't know squat, but that's not what I find intriguing."

"I don't follow you, Rex."

"It's not what she knows that's gotten my attention. It's who she knows, and I'm wondering how Robert Midew would react if something serious happened to young Ranger Kelli Katterman. That might change our, uh, negotiation with him a bit, and hell, save me some money in the process too."

"So, what are you thinking?"

"I'm thinking that a mine tour might be in order. That's what I'm thinking. We tell them that we've found evidence of an old Indian shrine deep in the mine, and then well, we'll let nature take its course. Just follow my lead, okay?"

"Okay," Digger replies, "but are you sure you're feeling up for this, Rex?"

"Yeah, I think I'll be all right. Just be prepared to move fast when I tell you to, understand?"

The two men return to Kelli and Rennie who are mesmerized by the huge equipment, large copper buckets, and ore carts scattered around.

"Sorry to hold you folks up," Rex says.

"That's okay, Mr. Trammer, we know we showed up unannounced and that you're a busy man."

"As I think about it, Ranger Katterman, many years ago our men came across something deep inside the mine that we've sometimes wondered about." He continues his lie. "We found a special chamber with very old Indian cave drawings and ancient-looking candles and ceremonial-looking stuff. Even found a carved-out niche that appeared to hold something, uh, special. We all thought it was a bunch of old Indian crap, and so we never told anyone about it. As you know, there's a lot of mumbo jumbo ghost stories up here on the Keweenaw. Anyway, if you and Rennie are interested in taking a look with us, I'll let you be the judge if it's something worth looking into more. How's that sound?"

"Wow, that sounds amazing, Mr. Trammer. Rennie, are you okay spending more time here?"

"Absolutely! Sounds spooky, but I'm definitely game."

Rex turns to Digger and says, "Why don't you get these folks ready with the appropriate helmets and jackets and fire up the cog railway for us. I think a tour of level seven might, uh, prove revealing."

"Right away, boss! Come this way folks, and we'll get you properly outfitted."

"This is so cool," Rennie coos. "I've never been in a mine before. How deep are we gonna be?"

"Oh, only about three hundred feet," Digger replies. "Level seven is the level where we give our tours for the public, but there are side tunnels at that level that go on for quite a way. I doubt much of it has been explored in years."

"Is there any artificial light down there?" Kelli asks.

"Oh yeah," Digger replies, "but only for a limited area. Years ago we ran electricity to help with mining operations and in later years for the public tours, but it only runs about a hundred yards now. After that it's pitch black."

After donning the proper gear, Rex and Digger lead the way over to the cog railway engine. It sits at the top of a long slope and provides a stunning view of Copper Harbor and Lake Superior.

"All aboard," Digger exhorts. "Next stop is the entrance to the Brockway Mine.

The descent down the cog railway is slow and plodding, but after several minutes they arrive at a large cave-like opening. It looks like a forbidding maw ready to swallow anyone and anything that ventures inside. Kelli thinks back on her classics studies in college. A line from Dante's *Inferno* flashes in her mind, "Abandon all hope ye who enter here." It was the inscription that Dante wrote above the Gates of Hell. Kelli privately shivers as they venture forward. They step into the opening in the earth where even the electric lights seem to struggle against the darkness within.

Rex looks over at Digger and nods at him to lead their guests forward. Digger provides his usual tour commentary for Kelli and Rennie about the veins in the rock walls and ceiling where copper ore was extracted. He points out old drills that were used and the iron trams that were loaded with copper ore.

"I'm surprised it's so damp down here," Kelli says.

Digger replies, "It's all ground water, and you see where the miners constructed gutters and sump pumps to move the water away from their work areas. Like I said earlier the Brockway Mine has ninety-two different levels and pretty much everything below level seven is flooded. I doubt anyone has been down there in seventy-five years."

Rex plods along slowly and stops every few feet to catch his breath and to try to ward off the white hot pain that is returning behind his eyes. Digger looks at him with concern, but Rex keeps motioning him forward. After about a hundred yards they reach an area that contains a side tunnel and a heavy iron door erected to support the rock ceiling. This is where the electric lights end and the tomb-like darkness begins. They all turn on the lights on their helmets.

"Just a little further," Rex declares as he nods an entreating glance at Digger. "I think the place we're looking for is just around the bend in the tunnel."

Kelli and Rennie venture forward several yards. "I don't see anything that looks like a shrine, Mr. Trammer," Kelli states, and it's then that she and Rennie hear the sound of the massive iron door screeching shut behind them with Rex and Digger on the other side.

"Oh no!" Rennie shouts. The only words that immediately come to Kelli's mind are those of the poet, Dante. "Abandon all hope ye who enter here."

Chapter 8

UPON ESCAPING TIPPY'S amorous clutches and avoiding getting the crap kicked out of me by her rude pal, Maurice, I spent the night at a peaceful motel in Traverse City. Surprisingly, I slept well through the night and awakened feeling refreshed and excited about spending time with Rennie. I thought long and hard about telling Maggie about the episode with Tippy and finally decided there's nothing to be gained by being totally transparent.

I mean, Maggie and I have a very honest relationship, and there's very little I don't share with her, but telling my wife about another woman putting the moves on me and having to use the Demon camera on her lover is not something that's easily explained. So, why even go there, right?

After breakfast I left Traverse City around nine o'clock and followed U.S. Route 31 through Charlevoix and Petoskey, both towns that I've enjoyed a lot over the years. After enduring a white-knuckle drive across the Mackinac bridge, I steer Pappy west onto U.S. Route 2 heading toward the towns of Manistique and Rapid River. The Upper Peninsula of Michigan is a pristine world and decidedly different from the lower state. It's far more remote and less populated. The road leads through mature forests with occasional vistas of Lake Michigan that are a balm to my eyes.

I spoke with Rennie earlier, and he explained that he wasn't sure when he and Ranger Kelli would get back to Calumet from their trip to Copper Harbor and Brockway Mountain. Knowing where he left the door key, and that he has a spare bed and a well-stocked kitchen is good enough for me. I'm just delighted that Rennie is so excited about his doctoral studies and his summer assignment with the Keweenaw park service. If I can be helpful to him by photographing some intriguing Chippewa artifact and spending time with my son, I'm more than happy to do it.

A couple of hours later I approach the Keweenaw Peninsula and drive through the towns of L'Anse and Baraga. I'd forgotten the large number of Native Americans living in this area and was surprised to see the L'Anse Indian Reservation and the Chippewa community center and tribal police station in Baraga. I recall my friend, Banks, saying that if I needed any help up here that his former marine comrade, Robert Midew, would be the man to see. Banks said his friend lived and worked in Baraga. I tuck that thought away for now.

Several miles later I arrive in the city of Houghton which is home to Michigan Technological University. The city sits across the Portage water-way from its sister city, Hancock, and together these towns form the largest urban community on the Keweenaw Peninsula. Fifteen miles after that I arrive in the historic town of Calumet, formerly known as Red Jacket, and my GPS guides Pappy and me to Rennie's apartment.

I exit Pappy and stretch my road-weary muscles. I don't see Rennie's car parked anywhere nearby so I figure he and Ranger Kelli are still out somewhere on Brockway Mountain. I grab my camera pack and my duffel and step onto his porch. The door key is right where he said it would be, and I juggle my bags and step inside. It's a nice apartment, and Rennie's kept it neat so far. I find the spare bedroom and stow my gear. Even though it's midafternoon, I'm feeling a little tuckered and decide to stretch out for a little nap. It'll also help kill some time until my son returns home.

The next thing I know I'm awake again and nearly two hours has passed and still no Rennie. I'd like to do some exploring in the area, but I don't want to miss him so I call his cell phone to see when he plans to return. No answer. I try again. No answer.

"Oh well," I say to myself. "I'm just glad he's gainfully employed."

I see a promotional brochure about the area on the kitchen counter and take a look for places to visit while he's gone. I notice that the Keweenaw National Historical Park and Visitors Center is nearby and decide to take my chances on finding interesting things to photograph. Because I usually take my camera equipment with me everywhere, I climb back into Pappy and drive the three blocks to the park. The first things I notice are the wonderful stone buildings that house the National Park Services offices and visitor center. The buildings were once the headquarters for the Calumet and Hecla Mining Company and almost look like large mosaics made of basalt and sandstone, with copper gutters and fittings. Then, of course, I see some of the now-derelict out-buildings that were once used by the mine to process and ship copper ore by rail. Finally, I see a ginormous snowplow mounted on the front of a train engine. It's like a giant wedge. I mean, I've never seen anything like this for snow removal before, but I get it because these folks endure three hundred inches of snow … every freaking year!

The sun is getting a little lower in the sky and casting dramatic shadows everywhere I look so I start snapping away. I'm so engrossed in the scene I'm framing in my viewfinder that I don't hear a person approach me from behind. I turn to see a wizened-looking woman who appears as old as Methuselah staring at me with milky, grayish eyes.

"Oh!" I say as I turn and see her. "I didn't hear you come up. Can I help you in some way?"

She continues to stare holding on to an old wooden staff for stability. "It's not me you must help," she declares. "Your loved one is in danger. You must go to the mountain." She turns to leave me.

"Wait, wait, hold on there!" I plead blocking her exit. "What are you talking about?!"

Her milky gray eyes somehow reflect an ancient wisdom. She looks deeply at my face. "I see you're a good man who has a heart to make things right in the world. Your loved one is in danger and needs your help. You must seek him in the mountain." She pushes past me with her staff.

"Wait, hold on, please!" I implore. "Are you talking about my son, Rennie? Where is he? What do you know? Are you talking about Brockway Mountain? What kind of danger? Lady, talk to me, will ya?!"

She walks up to me and places her crinkled hand on my chest. "Yes, you have a good heart," she breathes out. "Yes, your dark-skinned son and the young ranger woman. Seek the one who can help you. Look for them together under the mountain."

I stare back into her milky eyes and ask, "Who are you? Why have you sought me out?"

"My name is not important although many years ago I was called Nokomis … grandmother. There's much at stake. Much we must protect."

"But, I don't even know where to begin," I say. "I just got here a few hours ago, and I only vaguely know where the mountain is."

"Seek the one who can help you," the wise-looking woman repeats as she turns to leave again. I stare directly into the bright sun as she walks a few paces away, and then as if in a dream, I see her form dissolve into photons of golden light and then she's gone.

I stand there thoroughly stupefied and look around hoping that someone else saw what had just occurred. I was alone. I immediately pull out my cell phone and call Rennie's number. It rings a couple of times. No answer. I try again. Same result. Totally unnerved, I walk in absentminded circles. "Holy crap!" I say aloud. "There's a good reason why Maggie says I always get involved in major shitstorms. Not again, not Rennie!"

I walk back toward Pappy trying to grasp this dire warning from some old, disappearing woman. None of it makes sense, and yet in my core I know that she wasn't just some melodramatic apparition. I get into Pappy and just sit there trying to figure out what to do next. I call his cell phone again. Again, no answer. I start up Pappy and drive the three blocks back to his apartment praying that he returned while I went to the park. He's not home. I decide to drive to the park service's office to see if he and Kelli went there. I run inside and see a middle-aged ranger by the front desk. I manage to compose myself somewhat so I don't terrify the woman with my dread.

"Uh, hi," I say. "I'm Clay Arnold, and I'm here to see my son, Rennie Cotton, and Ranger Kelli Katterman please."

"Oh, my goodness, it is you isn't it Mr. Arnold?! Rennie said that you might be coming up to the Keweenaw. We're honored. Let me check."

She glances at the staff sign-in sheet. "Well, it looks like Ranger Kelli and Rennie checked out of the office earlier today for Brockway Mountain. It appears that they're still gone. We're about to close, but you're welcome to wait here for them in the vestibule if you wish."

"Thank you," I reply. "It's important that I speak with Rennie very soon. I've tried reaching him on his cell phone but haven't been able to get through. Do you think you could call Ranger Kelli's phone and see when they plan to return?"

"Well, we try not to bother our rangers when they're in the field, but for you, sir, of course."

The desk clerk finds Kelli's number in the staff phone directory and calls. She smiles as it rings and rings. "Sometimes phone reception around the mountain isn't great. Let me try again." She continues smiling and says, "Well, it appears that I can't reach her either. I'm sorry."

I get Kelli's phone number from her, thank her, and head back to Pappy. I mumble to myself, "What the hell do I do now? I've never been here before. I don't even know a soul up here, and I can still see that old woman's milky eyes and hear her dire words."

I drive back to Rennie's apartment and go inside to think. A moment later I'm jolted when my phone rings, and I pray it's Rennie. It's not. It's Maggie.

"Hi darling!" I say trying to keep my voice friendly and even.

"Well, I didn't hear from you last night, Clay, so I'm hoping your assignment in the Sleeping Bear Dunes area is going well."

"Oh yeah, it went fine," I fib. "In fact, the way things turned out, I was able to get away early. I'm actually at Rennie's apartment right now in Calumet waiting for him to get home from work."

"Wow! I hope you got some great shots and had some interesting experiences out in the dark under the stars."

"Oh yeah, you know me, great shots and interesting experiences," I repeat. "How are things at home?"

"Things are fine although both Tori and I are getting concerned about Mace. I think we all know that once you get in your mid-eighties, every day is a gift."

"Yeah, I know. Do you need me to come home?" I ask praying that she doesn't, at least not until I connect with Rennie.

"No, that's not necessary, Clay. He's not bedridden or anything. He's just grown old, and as much as he tries to hide it, Tori and I can see that he's declining."

"I know," I softly say again. "I'll be home in a few days, okay?"

I tell her I love her and ask her to send my hellos to Mace and Tori. Then, we hang up, and I'm left alone not knowing where my son is and the unsettling words of an old Indian woman reverberating in my ears.

Absently, I unpack my gear and empty the contents of my pockets onto the kitchen counter. I look at my cell phone and instinctively go to my text messages. That's when I see my friend Banks's, previous message about contacting his friend, Robert Midew, if I get into a bind up here. I decide that my not being able to contact Rennie and the spectral-like visit from the old Indian woman definitely qualify as a bind. I dial Robert's number and cross my fingers that someone up here has cell service.

Chapter 9

REX AND DIGGER RETRACE their footsteps a hundred yards through level seven of the Brockway Mine and return to its sky-bright entrance. "Every time I come out of that god-forsaken hole in the ground, I swear I'll never go back in. It just creeps the crap out of me, Digger."

"Aw it's not so bad, boss. I've kinda gotten used to being underground, and sometimes I swear I can hear sounds, like human or animal sounds. That's

kinda creepy, I admit, but most of the time when I do guiding tours it's just sorta peaceful."

Rex looks at Digger like he's from a different planet. "Yeah, I'm sure that ranger and her helper are feeling really peaceful right about now. C'mon, let's go back to my office. We gotta make plans."

The two men take the cog railway back up the mountain slope and ride the elevator up to Rex's office. He immediately pulls his container of pain pills from his desk and swallows two. "These things help, but not as much as they did a few days ago, Digger. This goddamn tumor growing inside my head is gonna get me if I can't do something quick, like getting that magic shell thing, and even then I'm not so sure."

Digger quietly nods his understanding. "Well, what do you want to do, boss?"

"Let's see if we can get Robert Midew back on the phone. Maybe if I offer to sweeten the deal, he'll have a change of heart."

"I think he made it pretty clear that money isn't going to motivate him to give up the secret of his people's sacred shell."

"I'm no longer thinking about money, Digger. I'm thinking about his being able to save the lives of that black guy and the young ranger he's gotten to know. Trading their lives for mine. Hell, if that doesn't change his mind, then nothing will. This brain tumor may have a huge advantage on me, but I'm not going down without a fight."

"Well hell, boss, we can't just let those two die in the mine. I ain't in this for killing anybody. Yeah, there's some oxygen and water down there, but once the batteries on their helmet lamps wear out, they'll be screwed down there in the dark. Naw, I ain't into killing anybody."

"Well, I'm not either, Digger, but their deaths will be on Robert Midew's conscience if he doesn't give in. That's something I can take to my grave. Screw 'em!"

Digger finds Robert's telephone number at the tribal council center and places the call for Rex.

"This is Robert Midew," the voice on the other end says. Digger hands the phone to Rex.

"Mr. Midew, this is Rex Trammer calling you." There's silence on Robert's end.

"Are you there, Robert? I need to discuss something with you."

"Yes, I'm here, Mr. Trammer. What is it you wish to speak about? I think I made it pretty clear when you were here that the Megis shell is not for sale."

"Yeah, yeah you did, Mr. Midew. I'm not thinking about money. How would you feel about a trade?"

"Are you speaking about the woman and the young man, Rex?"

"How'd you know about that, I mean, what are you suggesting, Mr. Midew?"

"Please, Rex, let's not play games, especially when lives are at stake. I told you before information has a way of flowing to me."

"Well, you're just a barrel of surprises, aren't you, Robert?" Rex's comment is greeted only by Robert's silence.

"Are you there, Midew?" Rex asks again.

"Yes, I'm still here, Mr. Trammer, but alas, I fear you won't be for very long."

"Is that a threat, Midew?"

"No sir, it's no threat, it's only a statement of fact. I take it your pain medication isn't working as well as it did before."

"How'd you know that?" Rex stammers. "Never mind … you already told me that information has a way of, uh, flowing to you. Whatever the hell that means! Now listen up, chief, and listen good! You either get over here with that sacred shell of yours and do whatever horseshit magic you can do to make me well, or those two young people will be buried forever where no one will ever find them. Understand?!"

"Yes, I understand, Mr. Trammer. It's their lives for yours."

"That's right, and don't go thinking about calling the police and raiding my place. I've got nothing to lose anyway, and it'll be your word against mine. I don't think those two will last as long as I'm willing to hold out. Come here and bring your precious Megis shell. Meet me here at the mine and brush up on your mumbo jumbo incantations because you're not getting those two kids back until I'm prancing around like old Walter." Rex slams the phone down.

"I guess I told him, didn't I, Digger?!"

"Yeah, boss, you told him alright. I wonder what Robert will do."

Meanwhile down in level seven of the Brockway mine, Rennie and Kelli have been hollering and banging rocks on the iron door ever since Rex and Digger slammed it shut.

"What the hell is this all about?!" Rennie shouts. "I mean, holy crap, did they do that on purpose and for what possible reason?" He continues banging on the door. "Let us out of here!"

Kelli reaches deep within herself to try to understand what Rex and Digger's motivation is for locking them under a mountain, and how to get themselves out of this awful predicament.

"Well, Rennie, I don't think that door closed by itself, and it certainly wasn't an accident. The question now is are they coming back, and if so when?

And, do we have enough oxygen down here and how long will the batteries in our lights hold out?"

"Good questions," Rennie replies getting some of his composure back. "If they locked us down here, we have to conserve whatever resources we can starting with one of us turning off our headlamp. No sense in using two lights at once. We should also look around to see what's been left down here that we can use."

"I agree," Kelli's says as she turns off her headlamp. "Let's see what we can find, but we should stay relatively close together so we both benefit from the single light."

The area of the mineshaft they now find themselves in is a long avenue that trails off into the darkness. The long avenue is some ten yards wide and extends well beyond the reach of their light. A side mine shaft runs perpendicular to where they are. They begin searching for anything helpful together. They see a couple of old water-cooled drills and iron tram carts. They see an old relic of heavy equipment sitting lifelessly in a large niche, and Kelli accidentally finds a rough-looking wooden box containing candles and stick matches. Although enclosed in the box, several of the matches appear moldy and beyond use. A few have potential though.

"Great find, Kelli! Hopefully they'll let us out of this hellhole before our batteries run out, but it's good to have those in case we need them. Let's keep looking, okay?"

Kelli and Rennie continue to search the mine shaft as best they can with one head lamp. Here and there they find bits of old copper wire, rusty drill bits, and heavy buckets. Not much else. They return to the iron door and began pounding on it as if that'll bring Rex and Digger to their rescue. A half hour later they both sit on the ground tired and dejected.

"Now I understand why Thomas Arrowsmith was so reluctant to call Rex Trammer for us, Rennie. Trammer certainly isn't a man who we can count on to do the right thing."

"Amen to that," Rennie acknowledged. "I still don't understand why he and that Digger guy would want to harm us. Makes no sense!"

"Since we're just sitting here, Rennie, we might as well turn off the headlamp to conserve the battery and try one of these candles instead."

He agrees, and after two failed attempts to strike an ancient match, he finally gets it to light one of their small candles. "What's that biblical verse?" Kelli says. "Better to light but one candle than to curse the darkness."

"Yeah, well, I'm not just cursing the darkness right about now," Rennie declares.

The two hapless captives sit in the dim light thinking aloud about their limited options when Kelli notices that the candlelight is shining erratically. "Looks like we have a draft coming from somewhere, Rennie. Look at the candle."

Sure enough, Rennie notices the candlelight dancing in a very erratic manner. "Well, hopefully that means we won't suffocate down here, and we have some ground water to drink, although no telling how potable it is."

Just then the candle light goes out, and Rennie is about to turn on his headlamp when Kelli suggests, "Why don't we take a moment to sit in total darkness to let our eyes adjust and use only our sense of hearing?"

Rennie privately thinks it's a silly idea but figures he can always turn his headlamp back on in a little bit. The darkness in the mine shaft is unlike any darkness the two have ever endured before. It's complete and relentless. Twenty minutes later their eyes have adjusted somewhat, but given Rennie's dark skin color, Kelli can't see him just a mere foot away.

"Well, I've had enough fun in the dark," Rennie states. "Do you want me to relight the candle?"

"Not yet," Kelli replies. "I want to know if we can hear anything else beside the sound of dripping water." They continue to sit in the all-consuming darkness with only the sound of air moving gently in their ears. One minute, ten minutes, a half hour passes with no light and very little sound. They both sit still, feeling only the beating of their hearts.

"Okay Kelli," Rennie says. "Let's throw some more light on our predicament. I'm gonna relight the candle."

Just then though Kelli touches Rennie's arm and says, "Wait! I thought I heard something!"

"Yeah, probably a giant vampire bat coming to suck our blood," Rennie jibes sarcastically trying to cast some levity onto their sorry state of affairs.

"No really, Rennie, I thought I heard something. It sounded like rocks shifting from something moving."

"Swell!" Rennie replies. "I suppose we now have a giant vampire bat walking around on the loose rocks!" Then he hears the sound as well, and his sarcasm morphs into fear.

"There it is again, Rennie," Kelli says, and they both instinctively stare in the direction of the sound.

"Look at that!" Rennie exclaims. "Is that a light way down there at the end of that side mineshaft?"

Sure enough, with their night vision fully restored now, they both see a very faint pale glow, barely perceptible, reaching through the total darkness and giving a ray of hope for another way out. And then they hear the sound of movement again followed by a primeval howl, and their hope turns to dread.

"What the hell is that?" Rennie beseeches. "It sure didn't sound like a bat to me."

"It sounded canine and large," Kelli offers, "but I sure can't imagine a dog being this far underground. It sounded like it was coming from the main shaft. I suggest we gather our stuff and head down the other shaft toward that glowing light. It doesn't seem likely that Rex and Digger will be opening that door for us anytime soon."

"I'm with you, Kelli. Let's stay close together. No telling what else we're likely to encounter down here." He turns on his head lamp, and they proceed into the jagged rock maw.

Chapter 10

"HELLO, THIS IS Robert Midew," I hear the strong voice say on the other end of the line.

"Hello, Mr. Midew, this is Clay Arnold calling you. I'm a friend of Banks, and I was hoping to speak with you if you've got some time."

"Banks, huh?! And how do you know him?"

I begin to answer his question when Robert interrupts and says, "Now I remember. You're Clay Arnold the photographer, right? You and Banks had

a little altercation with some nasty Russians about five years ago trying to save President Horvath's life."

"Little altercation doesn't quite describe what occurred, especially since we were trying to save my son, Bodie's, life, too, but yeah, Banks and I spent some serious time together."

"Well, you spent some time with a very special man, Clay."

"Yeah, and he says the same about you, Robert. Listen, I'm really sorry to invade your privacy, but when I spoke with Banks a few days ago, I told him I'd be coming up to the Keweenaw to visit my son. He told me about your serving together in the marines and said if I got into a bind up here that you're the man to see. He gave me your phone number, and I'm in a bit of a bind. So, that's the reason for my call."

"I see," Robert says softly. "Your son is the dark-skinned young fella working with Ranger Kelli Katterman, yes?"

"Yes, but how do you know that?" I ask highly surprised.

"Oh, information has a way coming to me," Robert replies evenly. "Listen, Clay, I was just getting ready to head out. There's something I need to tend to on Brockway Mountain. Why don't I swing by where you're staying in Calumet, and we can talk. Should take me about forty minutes to get there from Baraga."

"Sounds fine, but how do you know that I'm staying in Calumet, and how do you know where to find me?" I ask bewildered.

"Like I said, Clay, I hear things. I'll see you in a little bit." And then he hangs up. I stare at my phone in confusion, wondering how the hell this guy knows stuff that I barely even know.

The minutes drag on as I wait to see if Robert Midew really does know where to find me. I try calling Rennie's cell phone again without success. For the life of me, I can't figure out what's going on with him. I know he's a responsible young man, and if he's going to get home really late, I know he'd ordinarily call and give me a heads-up. I try calling Kelli Katterman's phone, too, but there's no answer.

I pace around in Rennie's apartment wondering what this Robert Midew fellow is going to be like. I mean, first I encounter a disappearing old Indian woman who tells me to seek the one who can help me find my son and Kelli, and then I speak with Robert, another Chippewa, who says that obscure information has a way of flowing to him, plus all of it seems to be leading us to someplace on, in, or under Brockway Mountain. I mean, this is some pretty weird shit, and I've got a feeling it's going to get even weirder before it gets better.

After several minutes of shaking my head in confusion and muttering to myself, there's a knock on the door, and I open it to find an impressive-looking individual. We both eye each other for some long milliseconds, and I show Robert in. When I say impressive, I don't mean that Robert Midew is really large physically or very wealthy looking, I mean that his very nature, his stature, and the look in his eyes reflect a certain prescience, a deep preternatural understanding of the core of things. We shake hands and sit down at the kitchen table.

"I have a problem," I say. "I think my son, Rennie, and the ranger he works with may be in trouble. They went out to Brockway Mountain earlier today to talk with some people about a sacred Chippewa relic that I'm sure you know much more about than I do. It hasn't even been twenty-four hours since he's been gone so I can't see what the police would be willing to do. Anyway, I'm concerned, and I remembered Banks's advice to contact you if I got into a bind."

"What else can you tell me?" Robert asks patiently.

"Oh yeah, I forgot to tell you about my running into a nice, little old Indian woman in the park who warned me that my son and his friend are in trouble, and to seek a person who could help me. I'm assuming that's you, right? Oh, and then the real kicker was when the old woman dematerialized before my very eyes. So you see, Robert. I have a problem."

Robert looks back at me with a knowing smile on his face. "We both have a problem, Clay, and we need to fix it before it's too late. Nokomis was good to warn you, although I may have to speak with her about dematerializing in public. We Midewin generally frown upon such blatant displays of, uh, sorcery."

I look at Robert like I just landed on the Planet Whatthefuck!

"C'mon," he says. "We need to go out to Brockway Mountain to confront the people who abducted Kelli and Rennie. I'll explain more to you on the way. I'll drive."

I collect my wallet, keys, and phone from the kitchen counter and grab my camera gear, then follow Robert's lead to his Jeep. I've got so many questions I don't know where to begin, so I ask the obvious one, "Are you serious about the sorcery?"

Robert looks at me and calmly replies, "Yes, Clay, and there are a few things that I can tell you and many others that are not allowed to be spoken to nonbelievers."

"Well, if Rennie and Kelli really are in danger, and we get them back safely, I'll definitely become a believer."

Robert smiles his all-knowing smile as he pulls onto Route 41 toward Copper Harbor. We drive past the old ghost towns of Mohawk and Phoenix without speaking, and then I say, "Okay enough silence, Robert, will you please tell me what's happening because I don't have a clue?"

"The owner of the defunct Brockway Mine is a petty man named Rex Trammer. Mr. Trammer has brain cancer, and he'll be dead within the year. He learned of our sacred Megis shell and its special healing powers, and he believes it can help him which is probably true. He and his assistant, a man named Digger Finn, recently visited me and offered my people $10 million if I shared its secrets. I declined his offer. So, apparently, he's found another way to get my attention."

"Abducting Ranger Kelli and Rennie, right?"

"Yes. He's aware that I took Ranger Kelli under my wing when she first joined the National Park Service staff as the education coordinator. She has a fine mind and a good heart, and I won't let anything bad happen to her if I can help it. Your son, Rennie, was just in the wrong place at the wrong time and got abducted as well."

"Swell," I say sarcastically. "So, are you prepared to meet their demands if it means we get Rennie and Kelli back?"

"First, we need to hear what they have to say and determine the strength of their resolve. The Megis shell is very powerful and has been central to our tribe's belief system since the beginning of time. It needs to be protected. Its powers are not something that should be easily given away, especially to men of bad faith. One thing's for sure, bringing the cops in now will not get us their freedom. Rex Trammer is a desperate man, and like the old Bob Dylan line goes, 'When you ain't got nothing, you ain't got nothing to lose.' Please follow my lead on this, Clay."

"Follow your lead?! If these bastards have my son, Trammer won't have to worry about the cancer killing him. I'll do it for him, and that Digger guy can decide if he wants the same treatment."

"I understand your rage, Clay, let's see if we can be smarter than that and get our young people back."

I stare out of the passenger's window fuming with anger. I haven't felt this much fear and rage since the Russians abducted Bodie and President Horvath five years ago. Now those feelings are back. "All right," I say to Robert. "We'll try it your way."

"Looks like we've got company, boss!" Digger shouts to Rex as he gazes out the office window. He sees two men exit a Jeep. "Looks like Robert Midew and some white guy I don't recognize. You want me to go down and let 'em in?"

"Bring them up here, Digger. I prefer to have these negotiations on my home turf."

"Yessir, Rex!" Digger replies as he watches his boss reach for more pain pills and wash them down with a tumbler of water.

Digger goes down the elevator and stands in the doorway of the shaft building.

"Digger, is Mr. Trammer around?" Robert says directly without any polite preamble.

"Yes. Mr. Trammer is upstairs in his office. He asked me to bring you up. Who's your friend?"

"His name's Clay, and he has business with you two also."

Digger eyes the two men and nods his head indicating for Robert and me to enter. The first floor of the shaft building doesn't look like it's been used in an active mining capacity in years. The three men ride the elevator seventy feet above the ground, and the door opens revealing Rex Trammer sitting behind his large wooden desk looking imperious with a large caliber gun resting by his hand.

"Well, well, look what the cat dragged in," Rex hurls tauntingly at Robert and me. "And who's this guy with you, chief?"

"I'm Clay Arnold, and if you have my son and the ranger locked away somewhere, I suggest you set them free immediately."

"Or what?!" Rex challenges as he grips the handgun and points it in our direction. "Did you bring the shell, Midew? I don't have much time to waste, ya know."

Robert deflects the question about the Megis shell and calmly says, "Put the gun down, Rex. We both have what the other one wants and shooting us isn't going to get you healed."

"Did you bring it or not?!" Rex demands

"No, I didn't, but it's not far away. Where are Kelli and Rennie?"

"Like you said, Robert, they're not far away." Rex points the gun at me and says, "I don't need both of you, Midew. What say I put a bullet in your pal, Clay, to emphasize how serious I am?!"

Robert stares intently into Rex's eyes and then closes his own.

Immediately Rex writhes in severe pain and drops the gun. He clasps his face in his hands, bellows in agony, and tries to reach for his pain pills.

"Had enough, Rex?!" Robert asks seriously, "Or, should we see if you can handle a little more?"

"You bastard, Midew, did you do that?"

"No, Rex, the cancer in your brain did that. I only fed it a little."

I look on in silent bewilderment by what I just saw.

Rex gasps and Digger runs to help him with the pain pills. A long minute later Rex manages to steady himself and says, "You son of a bitch, Midew,

I ought to just let you go ahead and kill me, but I swear those young people won't be far behind."

I stare over at Robert then reach my hand inside my pocket and feel a familiar shape. It's my Demon camera.

Robert looks at me knowingly and quietly says, "Don't do it, Clay. Remember you said you'd try it my way."

I release my grip on the Demon and reluctantly nod my acceptance. I sure don't know how he knows what I'm thinking, and it's more than a little unnerving. I remember our mutual friend, Banks, saying that Robert Midew was the finest warrior he'd ever known, and that he just has a way of sensing things. "All right," I concede.

"So, it appears we have a bit of a standoff, Rex. Why don't we do this? You show us where you've stashed Kelli and Rennie and let them go, and I'll at least temporarily agree to significantly ease your pain."

It doesn't take Rex long to reply. He knows how debilitating that last flash of pain was. "I can do that, Robert, if you give me your word as a Chippewa that you'll do as you say."

"You have my word," Robert pledges.

Digger assists Rex to his feet and helps him stagger to the elevator. The four of us descend to ground level and make our way to the cog railway.

The ride on the railway seems interminably long. Robert and I sit in front of Digger and Rex which is a little unnerving too, but at least Rex left his handgun on his desk. We finally reach the bottom of the slope and see the entrance to the Brockway mine at level seven.

"We enter here," Digger says. Digger reaches in the storage compartment behind his seat and pulls out miner helmets for each of us. "Here, put these on. The electric lights in the ceiling will illuminate the mineshaft for only about a hundred yards, then the lights on our helmets will be the only illumination we'll have."

I look inside the mine entrance and shudder at the thought of Rennie and Kelli being held captive in this deep, dark hole in the ground. I look at Rex Trammer and see that he's not thrilled about entering the mine either, but he doesn't have much choice. In some ways he's as much a captive to this subterranean world as his captives are. Going underground and freeing Rennie and Kelli is the only way to relieve his growing pain. We step inside and immediately feel the coolness of the earth as the mine engulfs us along with the last vestiges of natural light. I look at Robert who seems comfortable with the other-worldliness of the cavern. He senses my stare and looks back at me. "Don't fear the darkness, Clay, there's more than one source of light down here."

I really don't know what he's referring to, but at this point having seen an old woman dematerialize in the park, and watching Rex succumb to Robert's mental energy in his office, I know there's something going on that my mere mortal brain can't quite comprehend. I nod my acceptance again and try to remain focused on the uneven ground before us.

A few minutes later we arrive at the man-made terminus of the shaft. We see a large, closed, iron door stretching from floor to ceiling.

"They should be on the other side," Digger states. He approaches the door, grabs the long metal handle and wrenches it upward. Digger, Robert, and I pull on the handle to open the heavy door which screeches its opposition on rusty hinges. Finally we pull it open and peer into the eerie gloom.

"Rennie!" I shout. "Where are you, son?!"

We're greeted only by silence, darkness, and a shroud of demoralizing disappointment.

Chapter 11

MEANWHILE SEVERAL HUNDRED yards in front of us, Kelli and Rennie proceed cautiously forward. Every few yards they stop and look around at the rock walls searching for other side shafts and listening for whatever creature they heard howl in the depths of the main shaft. They hear nothing but ground water dripping off the walls and see no telltale signs of previous mining operations.

"Wow, look at this!" Kelli says as she examines a major vein of copper ore embedded in the rock wall beside them. Here and there they see large areas of green copper verdigris where oxidation has occurred. In other areas of the vein, the ore reflects its natural copper color when illuminated by Rennie's headlamp. And still in other areas they see another color of unexpected brightness.

"I think this is silver," Kelli surmises, "and from what I can see, it looks like the vein continues on for many yards. It must be worth a fortune."

"A lot of good that's going to do us," Rennie says. "I'd trade it all just to get us back into sunlight."

The hapless couple continues slowly forward as it appears that the batteries in Rennie's headlamp are beginning to lose power. He taps his lamp with his finger and the light surges but only briefly.

"Let's take a break and turn off the headlamp," Kelli suggests. "No sense in using any more energy than we need to."

They sit in the dark, and Kelli says, "Rennie, I'm really sorry I got you into this mess. Thomas Arrowsmith didn't try to discourage us from coming to see Rex Trammer, but it's clear he didn't feel positively about the man's character."

"There was no way you could've known we'd end up getting locked inside a mountain, and remember, I was pretty excited about gathering information for my doctoral thesis. So, please don't be too hard on yourself, okay? We'll figure something out. Oh shit, I just remembered that my dad's coming up here. He's always had a knack for getting into and out of trouble. Maybe he can think of something."

"You know, now that my eyes are adjusting to the darkness again, I think I can see that pale glow that we saw earlier. Take a look way down there in front of us, Rennie. Can you see it too?"

"Where, Kelli? Oh yeah, I think I see it now. It's pretty faint so the source of it must either be small or really far away. Let's keep walking toward it. It's got to be a way out, don't ya think?!"

"Only one way to find out. C'mon we've rested enough. Let's go find out."

The two trudge onward sidestepping rubble and depressions in the ground. The veins of copper and silver ore get even broader as they walk along, and they eventually come to a large cavernous room that looks like it's entirely comprised of copper and silver.

"Whoa! This is amazing," Rennie exclaims. "I've never seen anything like this. This space must be fifty feet across, and every inch of it is covered in copper and silver!"

"Not every inch," Kelli replies. "Take a look at this!" She points to a detailed series of ancient petroglyphs spanning a twenty-foot section of the wall. "I'm certainly no expert on Paleo-Indians, but these cave drawings appear to be thousands of years old. This is definitely an important find. Check this out, Rennie, it seems to depict a migration by ancient people, and look here, this symbol resembles a cowrie shell. It's the same thing as the Megis shell we've been hearing about at the park service office recently.

The two of them are so engrossed in examining the drawings and the ore veins on the walls that they almost miss seeing nine stone seats positioned in a circle around an impressive copper altar.

"Whoa!" Rennie shouts again. "The hits just keep on coming! This is incredible!"

They walk up to the altar and notice there's a carved niche on the far side. It's filled with silver bowls of herbs and what appear to be ceremonial objects … bones, feathers, shells, and stones.

"Some of these herbs appear to be somewhat fresh, definitely not something left here by Indians millennia ago," Kelli says. "What do you think, Rennie?"

"Seem fresh to me. I wonder if local kids sneak down here and smoke this stuff," he laughs.

"I doubt it, but it sure appears that this place is special and has been visited fairly recently."

"Well, maybe we just need to stay here and wait for someone to show us the way out."

"Maybe," Kelli offers, "but we have no idea how frequently anyone comes here, and they may not be very friendly if they find us in what appears to be a sacred place."

"Uh yeah," Rennie replies. "I guess we should be careful what we wish for, huh?"

The two of them are about to continue their trek onward in the direction of the pale light when they hear a sound that makes their blood turn cold. This time the canine howl is even louder than before.

"Oh boy!" Kelli shouts. "Turn out your light, Rennie. No sense in letting whatever that thing is know exactly where we are."

Without any further encouragement, Rennie switches off the headlamp, and the two frightened explorers grasp each other's hand tightly.

"I think next time I'm gonna to do a summer internship somewhere bright and sunny like the Bahamas," Rennie quips nervously.

"No shit!" Kelli curses uncharacteristically. "C'mon, let's see if we can back further away into the darkness behind those large boulders we saw." They take a few steps backward, still holding hands, and all of a sudden the earth beneath their feet is gone, and they tumble ass-over-elbows some twelve feet over an embankment and into a flowing waterway below.

They both sputter water out of their mouths as they resurface and quickly realize that they're capable of standing in the stream's four-foot depth.

"Kelli, where are you?" Rennie shouts. "Are you okay?"

"I'm here," she replies from a few feet away. "That was quite a drop off. I think I'm okay. How about you?"

"I think I'm okay too. Gimme your hand. I don't want us to get separated in the dark." The two of them clasp hands again and together stride against the stream's gentle current to what feels like a broad stone ledge. "Let's see if we can climb out of the water."

With a little effort they manage to exit the stream and huddle together for warmth. "Yeah, I'm definitely thinking the Bahamas next time," Rennie quips.

They stand still for a few moments collecting their equilibrium and listening in the darkness for the frightening howl of the large canine. All they hear is the sound of the stream and their breathing.

"Try your head lamp, Rennie. Let's see if it's still working."

Rennie tries clicking it on a couple of times without success.

"It's not working, Kelli. Maybe it will after it dries off a little, but generally electronics and water don't go very well together. And, I think our candles and matches are totally ruined too. Let's stay close to each other and see what we can figure out."

"Whew, this has been quite a day, and I still can't believe what we just discovered. Those cave drawings and that ceremonial ring are the stuff of dreams to anthropologists."

"Hey Kelli, maybe if we get out of here we can write a paper together for the scientific journals. *'The Katterman-Cotton Find and How We Lived to Tell About It.'* How's that for a title?!"

"Sounds great," Kelli says, "Especially the part about living to tell about it!"

They stand on the stone ledge pondering their limited options when Kelli says, "Hey look, Rennie! There's that pale light again in the distance, and it's providing a little illumination for us. I see a stone path. C'mon, let's see if we can get to it!"

"I'm game, especially before that big, howling creature returns!"

Chapter 12

THE FOUR OF US STEP through the heavy iron door and search the inside for Kelli and Rennie. They're nowhere to be seen.

"Damnit, Trammer!" I scream. "Where the hell are they?" I stride up to him ready to rip his throat out. He recoils in fear. "You'd better tell us where they are or I swear you'll never make it out of here alive." Then I turn on Digger. "And you too. Where's my son and the young woman?"

"I don't know where they are," Digger replies. "We left them here, so they must've gone deeper into the mine."

"Well, if you don't know where they are, you can explain that to the police. In the meantime we have to find them. How far does this mine go back?"

"Uh, we're not exactly sure," Digger says sheepishly. "It goes back quite a way, but there are places that have never been fully explored."

I look at Robert to see if he has any ideas. He stares into the blackness of the mine and then closes his eyes. "They have traveled far into places no white people have ever gone before."

"Yeah, and how do you know that?" I challenge with growing impatience. "Some more of your all-knowing sorcery?" I say sarcastically.

Robert looks at me sympathetically and replies, "We'll find them, Clay." At this moment, though, I'm not convinced.

Rex staggers again from the pain that's returned, and Digger says, "I'd better get him out of here."

"Yeah, good idea," I say. "You're sure pretty worthless down here, aren't you? You might as well go to your cozy little office and sit tight with your pain pills, Rex, but I swear if we don't get Rennie and Kelli back in good shape, I'll make certain that both of your lives are more miserable than they already are. Now get out of here, and if you even think about closing that door again, I'll kill you where you stand."

Rex and Digger slowly back up through the iron door, and Robert and I watch as they slowly move back toward the mine's entrance.

I turn to Robert again and say, "I'm sorry for the crack about your sorcery. I know you're just trying to be helpful."

"I understand," he replies patiently. "I'd feel the same way you do if it were my son, Clay, and Kelli is important to me too. C'mon, let's go. They've got quite a head start on us."

"Can you really sense where they are?" I ask hopefully.

"Not exactly where they are now, but I know where they've been, and we must hurry before they get further lost in areas where there's very little oxygen and no easy way out." He strides forward, and I hustle to keep up.

"How do you know this place, Robert?" I ask as we switch on our headlamps.

"It's a long story, Clay, and perhaps someday I'll tell you about it, but for now let's stay focused on the job at hand. I'll say one thing, though, from the way you acted with Rex and Digger, I can understand why our friend, Banks, would feel comfortable going into battle with you."

"I don't know, Robert, I'm just a photographer trying to make an honest living and looking after my loved ones and people in need."

We continue walking and finally come to the place where Rennie and Kelli found the rusty old mining relics and the wooden box that contained the candles and matches.

"Look here on the ground," Robert says as he sees the ruined wooden matches laying around.

"Were they any good?" I ask.

"Maybe some," he responds hopefully, "but this mine is vast and deep. Whatever they have probably won't last very long."

"And then what?" I beseech him.

Instead of answering my question he says, "C'mon, we must hurry. Getting lost in the mine is not the only thing that can hurt people down here. There is the Windigo as well."

"What the hell is a Windigo?" I ask with fear rising in me again.

"According to our legends, it's an evil man-eating spirit. No one who's ever met one has lived to tell about it, but I've seen grisly evidence of its existence."

"Oh, that's just swell. How will we know it if we see it?"

"Trust me, Clay, you'll know it. Let's go, we must keep moving."

The mineshaft seems endless, and eventually we leave the sites where any mining activities occurred. In some areas the stone walls rise to towering heights. In other places we need to drop to our knees and crawl through tight places.

"Look here!" Robert points. "I see two recent sets of footprints in the soil. At least we know for sure that they've been here."

"Good eyes, Robert! I would've missed those."

We continue on and finally come to the area where another tunnel veers off to the side.

"How do we know which way they went?" I ask.

There is only slab rock on the ground now so any signs of footprints are unrecognizable. Robert stands still and closes his eyes again. His furrowed brow suggests that he is struggling to discern which way to go. Finally he looks again at the side shaft and says, "This way. They went this way perhaps two hours ago, maybe longer. Come!"

We continue on for what seems like miles, but down here in the dim light with uneven footing it's probably no more than a mile. We stop to briefly rest, and then I begin moving again.

"Wait!" Robert commands. "We're entering a holy place, and we must pass respectfully."

"It all looks the same to me," I reply, and then Robert points to the stone wall behind me. With my headlamp I see what he means. Wonderful petroglyphs span a broad section of the wall's surface.

"These cave drawings were made by my ancestors many hundreds of years ago. They tell the story of our Chippewa people's great migration from the salt water ocean to where we dwell today."

"These are incredible," I say in awe as we examine the incredibly intact drawings. There are scenes of native villages, medicine men, hunting parties, battles with other tribes, and in the center of the scene is the unmistakable image of a glowing white shell.

"But wait, there's more," Robert states. He points his light into a large, adjacent chamber, and my jaw drops in amazement as I see that every inch of the room, floor to ceiling, is covered in copper and silver with stone seats encircling a large copper altar. I look at Robert and see him beaming with pride.

"Oh my God!" I say. "Are you serious?! This ceremonial site has been here under Brockway Mountain for all of these centuries and nobody has known?!"

"Yes, Clay, and the only nonbelievers who have ever seen it are you, Rennie, and Kelli."

"That doesn't mean you have to kill us now, does it?" I say in only half-jest.

"No, it doesn't, but if you were not a true friend to Banks, I might've given it a little thought."

I honestly can't tell if he's kidding me or not, but I know that he takes this holy place very seriously, and I am determined to respect his beliefs.

We approach the altar, and he shows me the niche containing the silver bowls of ceremonial objects. He lightly touches one of the bowls, and it glows brightly in the dim light and produces a low ringing sound as if it's been brought to life.

"I don't know what to say, Robert, other than I feel very humbled that you've showed this shrine to me. Rex Trammer would've literally moved heaven and earth to grab this if he knew it was under this mountain. I can certainly understand why you and the Chippewa people would be extremely reluctant to share it with the outside world. If we ever get out of here and you decide that you want a visual record, it would be my honor to photograph whatever you deem appropriate."

"Perhaps that may occur, Clay, but first we need to find your son and my young friend before misfortune befalls them. Come, we must go now, but be careful where you step. The ground beneath us is, uh, altered to dissuade unwelcome visitors. Please follow my lead."

I do so, and after several steps Robert stops walking and points. "Look here, Clay, look where the soil and rock have been disturbed by Rennie and Kelli's feet. There's a gentle stream below, and my guess is that they accidentally fell into the water. It's not deep, but there would be no easy way for them to climb back up here. We need to take the plunge too. I'm afraid that our headlamps won't work if they get submerged so try to hold yours well over your head when we hit the water. Ready?!"

"Uh, not really, but I'll follow you. I suppose it would be disrespectful to Native Americans if I hollered 'Geronimo' on my way down," I say nervously.

"You know, Clay, that's actually rather amusing!" And then he jumps into the dark water below, and I dutifully follow him.

Chapter 13

AFTER RIDING THE COG railway back up the long slope, Rex Trammer and Digger Finn slowly walk toward the mine shaft building and Rex's office. Once seated, Digger helps his boss get reasonably comfortable at his desk where he immediately reaches for his pain medication.

"How're you holding up, Rex?"

"Not great, Digger. This pain is growing intolerable, and I reckon I'm screwed with ever getting any

help from Robert. What the hell happened down in the mine? Where do you think that ranger and her pal wandered off to?"

"No telling, boss. It's a big mountain, and even though we did a lot of mining over the years, I'm sure there are many places that we never explored let alone mined. Those young people could be anywhere by now, and we may have seen the last of them."

Rex nods his head in agreement. "Maybe, maybe not. Like you said, there's a lot of places under the mountain that we never explored. That Clay Arnold fella threatened to kill me if we closed that iron door on them, but there's other ways to, uh, seal their fate."

"What are you thinking, Rex?"

"I'm thinking that we blow the whole damn mine entrance."

"Now wait a minute, boss, I told you I'm not into killing anyone."

"Yeah well, how're you gonna feel about spending the rest of your days in a federal prison? I know my life's not worth shit right now, but you have a lot of years ahead of you yet. You wanna spend the rest of your days bunking with some big jerk named Bubba or something?"

"No, I sure don't."

"Well, you might wanna think twice about Robert and his buddies walking away and telling the police about what we did. We can't get in trouble if they can't find the bodies. Remember, dead men tell no tales."

"Damn, Rex, you're serious aren't you?! What do you have in mind?"

"Hell yes I'm serious. If I can't get what I need from Robert Midew, then screw 'em. They can all rot in hell for all I care. Do you still have a supply of dynamite?"

Digger gulps, "Yeah."

"Good! I want you to go back down and rig the mine entrance and blow the crap out of it. We'll see how clever good ol' Robert is in digging his way out of a gazillion tons of rubble."

Kelli and Rennie venture forward along the path aided visually by the pale light that they see in the distance.

"How far away do you think the source of that light is, Kelli, and what could possibly be that bright this far underground?"

"Very good questions, Rennie, and I think getting to it is about the only way we're gonna find out. I do think that we're now on level eight of the Brockway mine, and remember we were told that everything below level seven is flooded?"

"Yeah, I remember, but clearly not everything is totally flooded. This path looks like it's seen a lot of wear over the years. Do you think the people who used the ceremonial shrine walked along this path too?"

"Again, a very good question. My guess is probably yes because I seriously doubt this path was listed on the website for the Keweenaw Peninsula's hiking trails. We've been walking for a while now. Why don't we take a break, okay?"

The two of them find a place to sit alongside the underground stream and cup their hands into the water to drink. "I'm getting pretty hungry, Kelli, you didn't bring anything with you to eat, did you?"

"Yeah, I have some trail mix, but I think it got pretty soaked when we fell in the water. Heck, it's better than nothing though." She pulls it out and the two of them snack on what they have. "You want to see if the matches are dry enough to light the candles, Rennie?"

"Sure." He tries to strike a match on the stone path, but the matchhead just smears. "That's useless."

"Here, let me try something." Kelli takes a matchstick and gentle rolls it in some dry sand that she finds. "Let's let it sit in the sand for a couple of minutes to see if it draws the moisture out."

While they're waiting Kelli sees something small jumping around and clinging to the cave's walls. "Crickets!" she chirps. "Cool! We've got cave crickets down here."

"So?! Should we call an exterminator?" Rennie says sarcastically.

"No, that's protein, my friend. We should eat some to keep our strength up."

"I'm not eating bugs!" Rennie protests.

"Suit yourself," Kelli chides as she manages to trap a couple in her hands and proceeds to chew on them. "Hmm yum! You oughta try some."

Rennie hesitates at first but then decides that starvation is a far worse fate than eating a few crunchy insects. "Hey, these aren't bad. Maybe when we get out of here we can start a snack food company," he jokes.

"Let's see if the match has dried well enough in the sand." Kellie gently rubs off the excess sand and strikes it against the stone path. It lights in the second strike, and she touches the flame to the candle wick. "And, it's just that easy, ladies and gentlemen. Let there be light!" she laughs. "And as long as we keep this flame going we'll be able to light the others when we need to."

"Pretty darn clever, Ranger Kelli. Did you learn that at the park service?"

"Nope! Just seemed logical to me, Rennie. Listen and learn, grasshopper!" she teases.

They eat their fill of crickets, wash them down with more stream water, and then move on down the path. Before long they come to another place that looks like a broad chamber and see more petroglyphs painted on the walls. They shine the candle on the wall and are mesmerized by the rich ochre and umber colors that they see.

"I can't get over these cave paintings. They're obviously primitive but really well done too. I just hope we get out of here to tell folks about them."

"Wow, look at this section," Rennie says with some trepidation. It's a scene of ancient Indians struggling to fight a large, ferocious beast. A number of the Indians lie on the ground mortally wounded, and the others have a bitter fight on their hands. "What the hell is that thing? Do you think this is what we heard howling? It doesn't look like a big canine to me."

Kelli examines it closely. "I've never seen anything like that before. I sure hope we never meet it. Let's keep moving toward the pale light and keep our voices low." They take a final look at the scene with the monster and quicken their pace. The path they follow meanders as it mimics the direction of the stream. In some places the rock ceiling above them reaches ten feet in height. In other areas they have to stoop and crawl their way through tight stretches. Every once in a while they see wide veins of copper ore intermixed with veins of silver and gold.

They turn a bend in the path and prepare to enter another chamber. They stop dead in their tracks.

"Oh my God!" Kelli exclaims as she directs the candlelight into a subterranean room totally comprised of luminescent crystals of various sizes and colors. Here and there they see huge quartz and amethyst crystals and scattered in the walls and on the ground, gleaming like stars in a night sky, they see a vast array of diamonds. Some are as big as Kelli's fist.

"Uh, Kelli!" Rennie stammers. "I think we've just hit the mother lode." Kelli nods her head in silent agreement. Rennie picks up two of the rough diamonds about the size of a golf ball and plops them in his jeans pockets. Kelli tries unsuccessfully to pick a large one out of the stone wall but has to satisfy herself with a diamond the size of a large hen egg she finds on the ground. She slips it into her pocket as well.

"Do you think we'd be able to find this chamber again if we ever get out of here, Kelli?"

"Probably, but next time I'm bringing a geologist's hammer, a shovel, and a cart!"

The two weary travelers sit in the middle of the chamber resting their feet and examining what could possibly be the the richest source of gemstones ever discovered.

"I'm really sorry I got you into this mess," Kelli apologizes to Rennie again. "My parents wanted me to be a doctor, but I've always loved nature, and I knew I'd never get rich working for the park service, but it's what I really wanted to do."

Rennie lightly touches her arm to console her. "Well, I'd say you're pretty rich now." He picks up another large gemstone and places it in her hand.

As they stand to leave they suddenly feel the ground above them tremble and the sound of an explosion overhead reverberates through the stone walls. "What the heck was that?!" Rennie shouts in alarm.

"Darned if I know, but it didn't sound good for us!" Kelli says. "My guess is that Rex and Digger dynamited the entrance to get rid of any witnesses … meaning us!"

"I think that's the most depressing sound I've ever heard," Rennie laments, and then they hear the baleful howl of a very large creature somewhere off in the darkness. "Make that the second most! Let's keep moving!"

Chapter 14

"WHAT THE HELL was that?!" I holler as the sound of a large explosion sends shock waves through the stream Robert and I are wading.

"Well, it appears that Rex and Digger took your admonition seriously about not closing that iron door on us, but it didn't prevent them from blowing up the mine entrance. I reckon they figure that if they can't have the Megis shell, then nobody can."

"Terrific! Now what do we do?"

"Now we keep searching for Kelli and Rennie. Once we find them, we'll figure something out. There's more than one way out of Brockway Mountain provided that blast didn't collapse any possible exits."

"So, how well do you know this mountain, Robert?"

"Not as well as I used to," he admits. "But there was a time in my youth when I got to know it very well. C'mon, Clay, we've got to make up some time."

We wade through the stream a ways, and then Robert says, "Over here, Clay, we'll get out here. There should be a path that we can follow."

We exit the stream, and Robert points to the stone path. "Look here. There's water from Rennie and Kelli's wet footsteps. At least we know that we're going in the right direction. We need to pick up our pace though."

"Hey do you see that? Where's that pale light coming from?" I ask. "I didn't see it earlier."

Robert evades my question. "We're now on the eighth level of the mine. It's a place no human has been in many years."

"Okay," I say, "but do you know where that light's coming from?"

"Yes, I believe so," Robert offers. "We need to hurry though. There are more dangers under this mountain than just being entombed for eternity."

"What the hell does that mean?" I ask in confusion.

Robert deflects my question. "C'mon, Clay, we need to keep moving."

Before long we come to a place where Robert bends down and sees a spent match. "Looks like they tried to strike a match here, but it was too damp. Hopefully they had success with others."

"I can't believe you're able to see these little things in the dim light. Good thing you told me to hold my headlamp above my head when we hit the stream. Hopefully Rennie and Kelli have more light than just that glow in the distance."

Robert continued leading us along the path. "If I recall correctly there's another chamber up ahead that you might find interesting." And, before long we come upon the cave paintings that Rennie and Kelli had seen earlier. My mouth drops open in awe when I saw the magnificently preserved images that Robert's ancestors had made. "Wow!" I exclaim, "And me without my camera." Then, I see the scene in which several of the ancients lay dead on the ground while others continue to struggle against a great hairy beast.

"What is that thing, Robert?" I ask. "You don't think it's still living down here, do you?"

"It's the Windigo I mentioned to you, Clay, and yes, it could still be living down here. It's the evil man-eating spirit that my people feared above all others."

"But what is it? It looks like a cross between a bear and a huge mole."

"It does indeed, Clay, but it's also very clever. One never knows when it will appear, and many of my people lost their lives trying to kill it. It's not just a myth." I nervously look over my shoulder. and quicken my pace.

A few minutes later we come to a bend in the path, and Robert says, "You're about to see something, Clay, that might brighten your spirits a bit."

"I hope you're talking about a way out of here, my friend, because the way you described that beast makes me doubt that anything can. We come around the bend and again my mouth drops open in wonder. It's the crystal room replete with gemstones lying everywhere. "Is this place for real?" I ask in amazement. "Are these really diamonds?"

Robert nods his head solemnly and replies with a smile. "They are, and they're of very high quality too."

"My God, Robert, you and your people have wealth beyond measure. No wonder you turned down Rex Trammer's offer of ten million dollars."

"Most of my people don't know of this place. Many of them would want to sell our treasure, and others of us know how great wealth can ruin one's soul and lead us astray from the teaching of the elders. You need only look at the greed that the casinos have brought. So, I sell a few stones that I collected many years ago, but only when we need to. The rest I've left for Mother Earth."

I nod my head in respectful understanding. "Whew, if Rex Trammer only knew what treasure was under the mountain."

"Yes, he and his people would've destroyed this holy place. In some ways the Windigo has been its protector, but it's an evil thing, not a friend to the race of humans. Let's keep moving toward the light. It's the only direction that Kelli and Rennie can go."

That's when we hear the long, baleful howl of a creature that stops me dead in my tracks. "Oh shit, what was that?!" I stammer aloud. "Please tell me that's not the Windigo." Again, Robert evades my question and keeps leading the way along the stone path toward the pale light and hopefully to my son and Kelli before the beast decides it's hungry for human flesh.

Digger returns to Robert's office and finds his boss with his head resting on his desk moaning in pain.

"Rex, are you okay, boss?" Digger asks with trepidation. He walks over to him and lightly touches his shoulder.

"No, I'm not okay, Digger, and these pain pills aren't doing squat for me."

"Do you want me to call an ambulance? You can't keep popping those pills if they're not working for you."

"Not yet," Rex replies about the ambulance. "Did you blow the mine entrance? I thought I heard an explosion, but I couldn't tell if it was the dynamite or the pain behind my eyes."

"Yeah, I blew it. I did what you told me. There's no way that Robert Midew and the others are gonna see the light of day again."

"Rex manages to nod his head. "Screw 'em, Digger. Hell, screw everything! Without that stupid Megis shell and Robert's help, I'm totally screwed too." For the first time in all of the years that Digger has known his boss, he sees a tear slide down his trembling cheek.

"C'mon, boss, let me take you to the hospital. We can't help you here." Rex finally relents and lets Digger help him to his feet. Rex looks out of his office window at the Brockway mining operations below. He doubts he'll ever see this scene again. His family's history on Brockway Mountain is slowly coming to a painful end.

Chapter 15

KELLI AND RENNIE continue walking along the winding stone path. Every once in a while when they round a bend they lose sight of the pale light, but it eventually returns like a beacon leading them onward … to what they just don't know. They just know that it's pointless for them to go back. The path leads them down a long slope with towering stalagmites and stalactites appearing on both sides like a stone forest. The candlelight on the toothlike rocks casts forbidding shadows that seem to move with each step they take. Downward they go, perhaps fifty feet below where they walked along the stream.

"I don't know about this," Rennie says. "It just seems like we're getting further and further away from the light of day."

"I agree, Rennie, but I just don't see where we have any other choice, and the good news is that we're not hearing that creature howling."

Rennie looks at his watch and figures they've been under the mountain for about four hours. "My dad's gonna be totally freaked that I haven't returned to my apartment by now."

"What do you think he'll do? Call the police?"

"I don't know. It hasn't even been twenty-four hours yet, and the cops generally won't consider a person missing until then. I told him you and I were heading out to Copper Harbor and Brockway Mountain, but we didn't know where we were heading for certain, so he can't possibly know."

"Yeah, I see your point. Even my mentor, Thomas Arrowsmith, wouldn't know that we're missing at this point, or that we even actually went to the office of the Brockway Mining Company to speak with Rex Trammer." She tries unsuccessfully to hold back a sob. "I don't want us to die down here, Rennie. I'm so sorry I got you into this."

"I know, Kelli, but I sure don't blame you. There was no way of knowing that Trammer and that Digger guy would be such assholes. But hey, let's look at the bright side; if we do manage to get out of here, we're gonna be pretty darn rich with these diamonds, and we'll write the best darn scientific paper since the opening of the Egyptian pyramids. And don't forget!" he says with levity, "We've got that cricket snack food company that we talked about forming."

That brings a laugh from Kelli, and she wipes away the tears on her cheeks. "Thanks, Rennie, for staying positive. Any other uplifting words you can offer?"

"Me? Absolutely! You've gotta remember that my dad's Clay Arnold, and what you don't know is that he's been in and out of more dangerous scrapes than anyone I know. Heck, about five years ago he and a man named Banks saved my brother, Bodie, and President Horvath after getting kidnapped by some really nasty Russians. Trust me, Kelli, if anyone can find us, it'll be my dad."

Kelli squeezes Rennie's arm for offering her reassurance. "Yeah, I remember that episode with your dad and the Russians. That was amazing the way that worked out! I guess we just need to keep walking toward that glowing light and hope for the best, huh?"

The path eventually levels off and again follows alongside a slowly moving stream. Thankfully, the rock formations change from their formidable, jagged, tooth-like shapes into basalt slabs with rich veins of copper and silver ore. They walk for another twenty minutes or so, and finally come to a fork in the path.

"What now?!" Rennie asks. "One path continues the way we've been heading, and the other one goes over that natural stone bridge to the other side of the stream. Seems like we can see that pale light coming from both directions."

"I don't know either, Rennie, but I need to rest a bit. My feet are starting to get pretty sore. Let's just sit down for a little bit, okay, and then we'll decide. We better light another candle, though, because this one's getting pretty low."

They sit down next to each other and put the candle on stable ground. Lulled by the rhythmic sound of the small stream, the two weary travelers fall asleep five minutes later leaning against a massive vein of copper with their heads resting on each other.

Robert and I continue walking on the stone path. Every once in a while Robert draws my attention to a scuff mark in the soil or a misplaced stone on the path indicating that Rennie and Kelli have, indeed, walked this way. "You're a helluva tracker, Robert, I wouldn't have given those things a second look."

"We each have our skills, Clay, and your fame is worldwide. I'm just some Chippewa fella living on the Keweenaw Peninsula."

"Uh, not according to our friend, Banks, and besides, down here I'd rather have a great tracker than a photographer any day."

We continue walking and begin going down the long slope through the menacing-looking rock formations. Down we go, further and further.

"This place just looks evil with these jagged, teeth-like looking formations," I say with a shiver.

"Indeed they do. Our elders say that these sta-lactites were originally Windigo that were turned to stone awaiting the day when they shall rise again and inherit their place in the land of the sun."

"Well, I hope that's not today, my friend. From what you said earlier about the Windigo, one is more than enough."

The path eventually levels off, and we continue walking beside a slow-moving stream. A moment later Robert abruptly raises his handing indicating for me to stop. He puts his finger to his lips motion-ing me to be silent. I watch as he closes his eyes to somehow comprehend what is in front of us. He turns to face me, and smiles broadly. They're just ahead.

Kelli hears us first and bolts upright with sleepy fear of the unknown etched on her face. Then, she sees Robert and runs to meet him. Rennie wakes up in the commotion ready to fight or flee whatever spooked Kelli, and then he sees me.

"Dad! You found us! Oh man, I've never, ever been so happy to see anyone in my life!" We both hug each other tightly.

"Remember, son, I've always told you that we stick together."

Kelli has Robert engulfed in a hug that surprises the man. "Robert, thank you for finding us. How did you know where to look? Thank you so much. You've saved our lives. I'm just stunned that you were able to find us!"

"You're worth saving, Kelli, and who's your young friend here?" he says pointing to Rennie.

Before she can answer Rennie says, "I'm Rennie Cotton, sir. I'm Clay's son and Kelli's intern. I'm so happy to meet you, sir. We didn't know how we'd ever get out of here."

"It's a pleasure to meet you, Rennie. Your father and I have been very concerned about the two of you. Are you both physically okay? Any injuries?"

"We're tired and frankly scared, Robert, but otherwise we're okay. Right, Rennie?"

"Yeah, we are now. I still can't believe that you found us under this huge mountain. I don't understand why Rex Trammer and that Digger guy would want to trap us in the mine. We didn't do anything to them that would warrant such treatment."

"It's a long story, but basically they wanted to trade your lives for something I have that Trammer thinks can extend his life. He's dying of brain cancer."

"But why not just ask you for your help?" Kelli asks.

"He did a few days ago, but he wanted to buy what I have, and I told him it's not for sale."

"What is it?"

Robert looks at me and Rennie and back to Kelli, and says, "The Megis shell."

"Seriously?!" Kelli exclaims. "The Chippewa artifact that has all of us at the park service buzzing about. Is it true what they say about it possibly having very special healing powers?"

"Yes," comes his frank response. "It's quite true, and it's a secret we've kept from the Light-Skinned race ever since they set foot on this land. There's more I may share with you later, but now isn't the time and place. We must find a way out of the mountain, and there are grave dangers that we may still have to face."

"You mean like that big, creepy thing that Kelli and I've heard howling a couple of times? That thing we saw on the cave painting killing your people?"

"Yes, the Windigo, the evil man-eating spirit."

I'm about to ask more questions when Robert holds up his hand again motioning us to be silent. He closes his eyes briefly and then looks behind us from the direction we'd all come. A moment later we hear a loud, grunting, snorting snarl, and the shadow of a huge hairy beast is projected onto the stone walls fifty yards away.

"Run!" Robert commands. "Run! Our lives depend on it!"

Rennie and I are so unnerved we immediately sprint across the stone bridge and run down a path. In the confusion Robert and Kelli bolt in the other direction down the path she and Rennie had been following. We're separated, and all of us are running like the wind. The Windigo has exceptional hearing and listens for its prey. He lumbers along with surprising swiftness and chooses the path that Robert and Kelli took. Rennie and I keep sprinting with adrenalin that only the fear of being torn to shreds can produce. We run, then jog, then walk a little. Then, we hear the distant grunting and snorting of the Windigo and run some more. We have no idea how far we've come, but we see the pale light before us and follow that beacon, praying that Robert and Kelli are okay.

Chapter 16

"RUN, KELLI, RUN!" Robert screams. "Run toward the light. It's the only thing that can save us. I'll try to hold it at bay as long as I can."

"Please don't leave me, Robert!" she beseeches. She casts a glance over her shoulder and sees Robert standing in the middle of their path awaiting the approaching beast. Totally out of breath Kelli ducks behind a large boulder. She looks in Robert's direction and sees a large shadow of the huge demonic

creature stretching across the rock walls. A moment later it stands in the center of the path thirty yards away from Robert. It sniffs the air, paws the ground with its huge, mole-like appendages, and steadily scrambles toward her friend.

"Windigo!" Robert bellows. "You shall not pass! You shall not feast on our bones and flesh! Slink back into your evil darkness! Begone from the bearers of light."

The Windigo moves slowly forward hurling its own bellows at the Chippewa human standing in his way. It stomps the earth and shakes its ravenous head from side to side. Even from this distance Kelli can smell the beast's putrid stench and sees it drooling with desire to kill and feast. It moves forward cautiously as if knowing the formidable opponent standing in his way.

"Be gone with your evilness. Return to your dark hole under this mountain. This is the ancient home of my people, and we shall keep it for all time."

But, the Windigo is strong and will not be denied. It bellows again with a snarling cacophony that sends shivers down Kelli's spine. She fears for Robert's life and her own. The creature jumps and snorts with determination. It cautiously approaches another few steps as if it recognizes a human that it has met before with unpleasant results. Then, it charges Robert. He extends his arms straight forward at the Windigo with his palms facing the evil one. Robert shouts with a voice that reverberates from the stone walls, "You shall not pass!" White hot rays of light shoot forward from Robert's palms, and the Windigo bellows in pain as the blinding beams sear into the creature's fur and flesh. Kelli is dumbfounded by what she's witnessing. The creature struggles against the painful surges of light but makes another charge. She sees Robert intensify his efforts even more with searing bolts of light now discharging from his eyes as well. The beast bellows in pain and withdraws into the darkness from whence it had come. Robert slumps to his knees, a spent warrior who has survived a mortal enemy.

"Robert!" Kelli yells as she runs to aid her friend. As she approaches him, she sees white light still emanating from his eyes, and then they slowly return to normal. "Robert, are you all right?" she pleads with fear as she kneels down beside the warrior. He stares at the ground and nods his head affirmatively but is still too physically spent to verbalize.

"Can you stand, Robert?"

"I need a second, Kelli, to catch my breath. The Windigo is gone for now, but it's strong, and I fear it will return. Where are Clay and Rennie?"

"They went down the other path when you yelled for everyone to run. Here, let me help you up."

Robert places his hand on her shoulder as he slowly regains enough strength to stand beside her. "We must go now before it decides to return. It's very powerful. Come."

"Which path should we follow?" she asks. "The one that we're on or the one Clay and Rennie took?"

"We must cross the bridge and try to catch up with them. The Windigo knows this realm better than anyone, and it'll not accept defeat easily." Robert slowly returns to his former stature, and they cross the stream, both of them casting cautious glances over their shoulders.

"How did you do that, Robert? How did you create those beams of light from your palms and eyes? That's not humanly possible! Is that something that the Megis shell has empowered you to do?"

A brief smile appears on his face as he looks at Kelli. "Yes," comes his singular reply.

"But how? That's the stuff of science fiction and fantasy, not real life!"

"There's more than one reality, my young friend, and that is all that I can share with you now." With his strength returning, he appears to be his former self, and they renew their pace to find Clay and Rennie.

"That's all you're going to tell me? And what the hell is that thing? How does it even exist?" she beseeches her Chippewa friend.

He deflects her question. "There is little else I can share with you now. As to how the Windigo exists, my people have always believed that the sleep of reason creates monsters. Come now. We must reach our friends, and then I need to rest some more."

They move forward on the path, and Kelli shakes her head in total confusion as Robert's words remain with her, *"The sleep of reason creates monsters …"*

Rennie and I both bend forward with our hands on our knees. We're exhausted from running, and we have no idea what fate has befallen Robert and Kelli.

"Are you okay, son?" I ask Rennie.

"Yeah, Dad, I think so, but what was that thing? I can't imagine how Kelli and Robert could've survived it. I'm really scared, dad."

"That makes two of us, Rennie, and I have no idea what that ugly creature is. It's certainly not anything I've ever been aware of except for seeing it on that ancient cave painting. We've got to figure out what we do now. I know Robert wants us to continue toward the pale light, but I don't know what the hell we'll do when we reach it, if we reach it. Right now I just want to find a place to hide out for a little while and rest. I'm exhausted, son."

"Me too, Dad, and I can't tell you how really sorry I am you got into this mess."

"I know. This certainly isn't something that you or anybody could've anticipated. Let's just chalk it up to one more, uh, adventure that we probably shouldn't share with your mom, okay? She already thinks I get involved in way too many shitstorms."

We continue quietly walking along this new path listening for any sound other than dripping water. Rennie spies a large boulder resting against the cave wall and looks behind it. "Dad, there's a shallow alcove behind this big rock. I think it's probably large enough for the two of us to squeeze into. Wanna hole up here to rest?"

I look around in all directions, and I'm honestly not quite sure what we should do. On the one hand Robert thinks our getting to whatever is shining that pale light is really important, but Rennie and I are both physically and emotionally drained, and this alcove looks like it could provide us some protection from the Windigo or any other large predator that could be lurking under the mountain. Then, we hear the baleful howl of a large animal.

"Uh yeah, let's hide out in here," I agree.

"What if that nasty beast comes though? We'd be trapped in here."

"Well, Rennie, I did bring the Demon camera with me, and I won't hesitate to use it. Why don't you try to get some sleep, and I'll keep watch, okay?"

And that's what we do. Rennie is so exhausted that he falls asleep within a few minutes. I peer out of the alcove's opening, hoping we don't need to make a run for it again. There's virtually no sound, and the air is still. The pale light provides adequate illumination for me to see. I stay on guard, but within a matter of minutes my eyes begin to close and my chin droops to my chest. Overcome with exhaustion, I fall deeply asleep under a mountain that's home to a savage monster with no known way out.

And then I dream. In my dream I see a young Indian boy walking along a rocky lakeshore with a wolf pup at his side. They find a very unusual white shell that glows supernaturally. The boy and wolf take it home to his grandmother who, in turn, shows it to their chief. There's a great tribal feast, after which the boy and his wolf are led away to this very mountain by the tribe's healers. Then, the next thing I dream is the boy talking to me directly, and he's saying, *"This mountain is sacred, but you will only be safe if you follow the light and listen to my spirit-guide. If you do not, you will perish in the jaws of the Windigo."*

I jolt upright from my dream and realize that I had fallen asleep. I nudge Rennie awake and say, "C'mon, son, we need to keep moving."

Rennie stretches and wipes the remnants of sleep from his eyes. We carefully look and listen as we emerge from the alcove and shimmy past the large boulder. It appears safe so we swiftly but silently walk along the path. I see the light glowing in the distance and remember my dream about the boy, the wolf pup, and the bright shell. I remember it as clearly as any dream I've ever had.

Chapter 17

"HOW MUCH FARTHER, Robert? I'm beginning to feel numb. Do you know where we might find Rennie and his dad?"

"I know you're very tired, and I'm very proud of how well you've kept up so far. You have the heart of a Chippewa, Ranger Kelli, but we need to keep moving along this path. It's been a while since I walked under the mountain. In my youth I came here often to learn to face my fears. I believe

this path will converge with Rennie and Clay's as we get closer to the source of light. If necessary, I'll carry you, but we need to keep moving before the Windigo senses we are weak and defenseless."

"It can actually sense things like that?" Kelli asks skeptically.

"Indeed it can!" Robert replies. "In my world, things are different than in yours. You must remember that the Windigo is part beast and part spirit. It has all of the senses that other animals possess like hearing, smell, and taste, etc., but as a spirit its sixth sense can perceive things in ways very unfamiliar to humans. In fact, it probably knows where we are this very moment. It's deciding if its strength is greater than mine."

"Are you serious?!" Kelli asks incredulously. "That big, hairy, smelly thing that looks like a cross between a giant mole and a bear also has a sixth sense? So, Rennie and I never would've made it out of here alive if you hadn't come for us, right?"

"Probably not," Robert says somberly. "And, we're not out of the woods, I mean, mountain yet! Let's keep going. I know you're tired, but there's something I wish to show you and someone I want you to meet."

"Down here? Five hundred feet underground? You want to introduce me to someone? You're not serious, Robert."

He smiles and nods affirmatively. "This mountain holds many secrets, Ranger Kelli! I wish you could learn them under less threatening circumstances, but perhaps you'll remember them best faced with this adversity."

"Oh swell!" she mutters sarcastically. "Look Robert, I don't mean to be disrespectful, but Rennie and I came out here looking to interview people who might know something about the Megis shell. I get that you didn't feel comfortable sharing important secrets about your culture with me previously, but there's been so much commotion going on in our office about this amazing Megis shell that I wanted to see if I could uncover some fresh details from folks living around Brockway Mountain. I never dreamed in a million years that Rex Trammer and Digger Finn would bury us alive. And poor Rennie, my God, I wish I'd never brought him along. He's such a great guy and deserves much better than this insanity. Heck, we could be buried under a mountain of bureaucratic paperwork at the office instead. It wouldn't be fun, but at least nothing there would try to eat us!"

"I understand, and I'm very sorry for all of this turmoil too, but I can see into Clay and Rennie's hearts and into yours as well, and if we have to go through this trauma, I'm heartened that we're going through this life-experience together. Ours is a convergence of spirits, and we will all be forever linked." He places his hand on her shoulder. "C'mon, we can do this together."

They continue walking along the path that feels endless. Here and there they see rich veins of copper and silver stretching before them in a colorful array. They walk for about fifteen minutes, and then Robert stops abruptly and closes his eyes, deep in thought.

"When we go around this bend in the path, we will come to a chamber where you will see wondrous things. I hope you'll keep an open mind. The knowledge brought by the Light-Skinned race is impressive indeed. Who and what you are about to meet will help you understand that other realities do, indeed, exist.

Kelli gulps with trepidation of the unknown, but she believes that Robert will keep her safe. They make the turn in the path and enter a stone chamber that has no adornment like the others they've seen. In the dim light Kelli sees a placid pool of water in the center of the chamber and the back of a seated figure wrapped in a woven blanket. They approach.

"Nokomis!" Robert calls out. "Grandmother, I've come to see you, and I've brought a weary friend."

They walk closer, and Kelli sees a wizened-looking old woman sitting calmly before the pool of water. Her braided hair is silver. Her skin is wrinkled revealing the ravages of time, and her eyes are milky gray and sightless.

Nokomis turns her head toward them. "Ah, Ahmik, hello my grandson, and who is this that you've brought to our sacred chamber?"

"This ranger is Kelli Katterman, but you already know that, don't you?"

She smiles and says, "Come child, come sit with me by this water so we may look into this pool together."

Kelli is a little shy at first, but Robert motions her to comply. She steps forward and sits cross-legged with the ancient-looking woman.

"I'm Kelli, ma'am, I'm pleased to meet you," she says not knowing what else to say in this situation.

Nokomis extends her hand to feel Kelli's forehead and then drops it down over her heart. "Ah, I see why Ahmik considers you a friend."

Kelli breathes a sigh of relief and looks into the old woman's milky eyes. "Are you totally blind, grandmother?" she asks. "How do you find your way around down here?"

"Yes, my eyes are sightless now, but over many years I have learned to channel my senses in a different way. And this pool allows me to see into the heart of things."

"I don't know what that means, Nokomis." Robert remains silent. The two women continue speaking. "So, you are the education ranger who teaches people about the Keweenaw. I see that you have made diligent efforts to share the ways of the Chippewa to the Light-Skinned race. I see that you're confused by what the Megis shell enables us to do."

"I am, and meeting you under this mountain raises many more questions in my mind. How is this all possible?"

"It's possible because we believe, and because we have followed the teachings of our Anishinaabe elders over many centuries. Is that not true, Ahmik?"

Kelli turns to Robert and asks, "Is Ahmik your Chippewa name?"

Robert nods his head in acknowledgment. "In today's world I am called Robert, but our people know me as Ahmik. Yes, Nokomis, we are members of the Midewin, the Grand Medicine Society of the Chippewa people. With the Megis shell as our guide and the riches of the mountain, we have protected our people. Now the question becomes, is it time to share what we possess with those who do not share our beliefs?"

Nokomis grasps Kelli's hand and says, "Look with me into this pool of water. You need only think about what you wish to know. The pool will reveal some, but not all of the answers. There are certain mysteries that must be experienced in order to know the final outcomes."

Kelli looks at Robert for clarification, but he stares intently into the pool of water and then closes his eyes. Kelli stares into the placid pool as well, and the waters begin to swirl, slowly at first then faster, creating what looks like a spiral galaxy of bright stars. Kelli closes her eyes and thinks about escaping the mountain. She opens them again and sees the glowing Megis shell hovering over the water. She then sees the promising image of an exit from the mountain into life-giving sunlight, but something is blocking the way. It's the Windigo.

"Oh no!" she says aloud. "The beast is blocking our way out. It appears even larger than it did before."

"Yes," Robert says somberly. "It appears that the Windigo is growing more confident. That does not bode well for us."

Kelli thinks about Rennie and Clay and wonders if they're safe. The waters swirl again, and she sees the two of them lost in the other tunnel slowly wandering in their direction. Then, the waters swirl again and the floating Megis shell pulsates with vibrant energy. She sees the Windigo blocking their path to where they are.

"Oh no!" she says painfully. "They'll never make it to us."

"Have faith, my friend," Robert says to her. "My spirit guide will help show them the way."

"Your spirit guide? What's that?"

Robert answers her question by pointing into a dim corner of the stone chamber. Kelli looks to where he's pointing and gasps when she sees a pair of glowing eyes peering at her from the darkness.

"Grey, come!" Robert says warmly. "Come say hello to our friend, Kelli."

A moment later the largest canine that Kelli has ever seen emerges from the shadows and stands by Robert. He nuzzles Robert's hand and leans his rich, grey flank against Robert's leg. It's twice the size of any German Shepherd that Kelli's ever seen, and its eyes reflect a certain unknowable wisdom that she didn't think was possible.

"Grey, go to Kelli," he directs, and the massive canine strides to meet this new human. Kelli stands stone still while Grey sniffs her fully to remember her scent … her hands, her feet, her crotch, her clothing. He finally rests his face between her knees and wags his tail.

"I think he likes you," Nokomis says. "He's not like that with many humans, including Chippewa."

"He's just a great judge of character, aren't you, Grey?" Robert says fondly. The great beast prances in circles and sits between Nokomis and Kelli by the pool of water.

"So, this is your spirit guide?" Kelli says. "He looks like a big, playful baby to me," she says with growing comfort. Grey barks and rests his head on Kelli's thigh. She scratches him behind his ears, and he responds with a satisfied moan.

"So, now what?" Kelli asks.

Robert replies, "Grey, find our other friends! Bring them to us, but be wary because the Windigo is present and growing in strength." Grey reacts with a savage growl that unnerves Kelli at first, but then he nuzzles her hand again.

"Find them, Grey!" The huge canine stares into the pool of water, and it begins to swirl and change color. An image of Rennie and Clay appear in a dimly lit tunnel. Grey barks again and exits the chamber at full speed.

"Be careful, my friend!" Robert calls after him. He looks at Nokomis with grave concern etched on his rugged face.

Chapter 18

RENNIE AND I CONTINUE our cautious trek along the tunnel. The pale light in front of us appears to be growing brighter with each turn we make on the path. Neither of us speaks loudly because we fear that the Windigo will hear us. We don't know how far we have to go, but we know that returning from where we came is not an option.

"How're you holding up, son?"

"Well, I'd be lying if I didn't say that I'm tired, scared, and hungry, Dad, but it sure helps having you here. I just hope that Kelli and Robert are safe."

"Yeah, me too, but I have a feeling that Robert will be safe no matter what. I don't know if I told you that my friend, Banks, said that he and Robert served together in the marines. He said that Robert was the best warrior he'd ever known."

"Well, if that's the case, I'm darn glad Kelli's with him, and I'm darn glad that I'm with you, too, Dad."

I give his shoulder a fatherly squeeze. "I'm not much of a warrior, Rennie. At my age I prefer to avoid conflict."

"Maybe not, Dad, but I'd never bet against you either. Heck, you and Banks kicked the crap out of the Russians, and we've both been through some crazy times together. Plus, you always have your Demon camera handy, right?"

I instinctively reach my hand inside my pocket to confirm that and feel a sense of reassurance by the Demon's presence. "We're not going down without a fight. That's for sure!"

Then, we hear the sound of a loud canine howl. It reverberates from the tunnel's walls sending small amounts of dust cascading around us.

"Not again!" Rennie gulps. "Whatever that thing is, I pray it's not the Windigo." We walk forward several more yards and stop dead in our tracks. A pair of glowing eyes greets us midpath about twenty yards in front of us. A chill goes down both of our spines. It walks slowly toward us, and I reach my hand in my pocket and pull out the Demon camera. I have it set to kill. Rennie steps behind me, and we prepare for the worst.

I'm about to fry his ass with the Demon, but instead of charging us, the great grey canine sits down in the path and proceeds to wag his tail.

"What the hell," I mutter. "He seems friendly," I say to Rennie. That's when we smell a horribly putrid odor and hear another sound behind us that sends an even greater chill down our spines. We turn and see the Windigo lumbering at us from fifty yards away. The large wolf in front of us barks loudly as if beckoning us to come. I figure, if we're gonna die I'd rather take my chances with a friendly looking wolf than a huge, nasty, mole-bear-thing that I know wants to gobble us up. We take off running forward and the wolf sprints leading the way. Horrific grunts and snarls thunder off the stone walls. I briefly glance over my shoulder to see where it is. "Shit! It's gaining on us, Rennie," and we run as fast as we can. I know it's a matter of time before it reaches us.

"Run, Rennie! I'm making a stand here!"

"I'm not leaving you, Dad," and he pulls up short too. The Windigo slows its pace as if deciding what it wants to do next. It comes within ten yards, and that's when we see a flash of grey fur go streaking past us, and the huge wolf leaps onto the Windigo's back and head tearing at it with a primal viciousness that I've never seen before. The sounds of the snarls and gnashing of teeth are terrifying. Rennie and I draw closer to the melee, and I extend the Demon in front of me. The Windigo manages to throw the wolf off its back, and it tumbles to the ground with a heavy thud. The wolf is stunned and wounded, but he still has fight in him, and he prepares to leap at the Windigo again. The evil beast is about to charge the wolf with what will surely be a deadly attack when I discharge the Demon camera. An angry blue arc of electricity engulfs the creature, and it bellows in pain and surprise. I smell the rancid odor of burnt fur and discharge the Demon a second time. The Windigo bellows again and stomps the earth in violent rage and frustration. It begins to come at me this time, and the wolf leaps on it with his last burst of energy. He clamps his massive jaws on the Windigo's throat and tears at its flesh. The Windigo is too large and strong, though, and it shakes the large wolf free and prepares to trample it. I discharge the Demon a third time, aiming the bolt of blue electricity at its hideous face. The evil being shrieks a blood-curdling wail and recoils in primal pain. Finally, it slowly slinks back into the shadows to nurse its wounds. The sound of its wails recede in the darkness. It's gone for now.

Rennie and I lean on each other for physical and emotional support. "Are you okay, son?"

"Yeah, I'm all right, Dad. How about you? Thank God you had the Demon or we'd all be goners."

We look at the wolf laying on his side. He's breathing heavily and has a deep gash along his flank. We slowly approach him, and his eyes meet mine. He voices a yelp, and his huge tail thumps the ground in amicable twitches.

"He needs our help, Rennie," I say as I slowly approach the fallen warrior. "There, there," I say as I kneel beside the large wolf. "Easy now," I say. "We're not going to hurt you." I ask Rennie to go to the nearby stream and fill my hard hat with as much water as it will hold. He does so and hurries back. I put some water on the wolf's muzzle and carefully wash the wound on his side. Rennie goes back for more water, and I repeat the process. The wolf lies still as I cleanse his wounds, and his panting begins to ease. Rennie and I sit next to the great animal and thank him for saving our lives. His eyes meet mine, and he gently places his forehead against my thigh in response. A few minutes later the wolf stands and manages to take a few feeble steps. Rennie and I both gently stroke the great creature and lead him over to the stream to drink. My son and I marvel at the size of this magnificent creature but even more at the wolf's apparent intelligence.

After refreshing himself with water, the grey wolf sniffs both Rennie and me and begins walking down the path toward the light. He stops and turns toward us and barks as if beckoning us to follow him. He waits for us, and Rennie and I join him, and we walk with the wolf between us. The path ahead is reasonably level and remarkable with its rich veins of copper. Here and there we notice rough diamonds embedded in the dark walls like stars in the night sky. For the first time I notice what look like nuggets of gold. The richness of this cave system is beyond belief, and I wonder if we'll ever get an opportunity to tell anyone about it.

Some fifteen minutes later the three of us approach a bend in the path, and the wolf barks. We make the turn, and our spirits soar as we see Robert and Kelli standing alone at the entrance to a cavern with a pool of water in the center. The wolf runs up to Robert who greets him warmly, and Rennie and I hug Kelli with a major sigh of relief.

"Oh man, are we glad to see you guys!" I effusively exhale. "I never thought we'd ever see you again. The Windigo almost got us, and if it weren't for this wolf, we'd be dead."

"Robert, where's your grandmother?!" Kelli asks with confusion etched on her face. "She was here just a minute ago."

Rennie and I wonder what she's talking about because it's only the four of us plus the wolf in the chamber. Privately, I wonder if Kelli is in a state of shock from everything that's happened since Rex and Digger slammed the iron door shut.

I look at Robert and ask, "What's she talking about?"

He smiles and says, "Do you remember the old woman you met in the park? The one that kinda dematerialized before your eyes?"

"Uh, yeah!? She was here?"

"Yes."

"And?" I ask him looking for more clarification.

"Well, grandmother is a little unique. Some might even call her a little quirky," he deadpans.

"Uh, Robert, disappearing is more than just a little quirky!" Kelli insists. Rennie looks at all of us like we're nuts.

"I know," Robert acknowledges. "I've known her all my life, and I guess I've just gotten used to her unusual way of coming and going."

"Huh?!" Rennie and I say in befuddled unison. "And, this wolf! I've never seen such a magnificent creature, Robert, and we wouldn't be here if it weren't for him."

"Believe me, I know, Clay. I raised him from a pup, and he's been my spirit guide ever since."

"One of these days, Robert, I'd really like for you to explain to me what the heck that means because I'm at a total loss for words for everything that you've shown and told us."

"Well, if you're at a total loss, Clay, I suppose it wouldn't hurt to show you one more thing." Robert closes his eyes, and when he reopens them, the Megis shell has risen from the pool of water and glows majestically before them.

"What the …" I begin. "Is this the source of light we've been following … the Megis shell? This the artifact that everyone's been so frenetic about?"

"Hmmm," Rennie says. "I thought it would be larger."

Instead of being insulted, Robert erupts with a hearty laugh. "Well, looks can be deceiving, Rennie!" And to prove his point the Megis shell swells to ten times its size with an illumination that is nearly blinding. We all step back a few paces and marvel at its magnificence.

"Grey, come!" Robert commands, and we watch as Robert closes his eyes and somehow causes rays of healing light to emanate from the Megis shell and surround his spirit guide in a warm, curative glow. A few moments later the glow is gone, and the Megis shell dips back into the pool of water.

"Feeling better, Grey?!" he asks, and his canine spirit guide jumps around like a young pup, totally healed.

Rennie, Kelli, and I stare at Robert and Grey incapable of muttering a word.

Finally, Kelli says, "How's that possible, Robert? How'd you do that?"

"Practice, practice, practice!" he laughs in an effort to deflect Kelli's questions, and then he gets very serious. "Perhaps there'll be time for me to answer your questions later, Kelli. We're getting closer to an exit from the mountain now, but the Windigo is far from defeated. It'll do everything it can to stop us. We must leave this sacred chamber now and take our chances. Come, my friends, we must go and face our fears."

"Swell!" Rennie jibes. "More fear-facing! That's just swell!"

T HE FIVE OF US WALK ALONG a stone path in areas that look like nothing we've seen before. The ceiling above us must reach seventy feet or more in height, and waterfalls cascade down great outcrops of basalt and iron ore. It's a wondrous view, one that probably hasn't changed much in thousands of years.

"Many years ago when I was a boy," Robert recalls, "our Midewin healers brought me here from

our village to learn the ways of the Megis shell. We lived above the mountain, but we studied the ancient teachings of our prophets and learned the lessons of the Megis shell in sacred chambers under the mountain. I recall this place well because my wolf pup and I would often play in these waters. That was before we grew to know of the frightening dangers of the Windigo."

"Why now?" I ask Robert. "Why have you decided that now's the proper time for you and your tribe to present the powers of the Megis shell to the world?"

"Who says we've decided that?!" he frankly replies. "Look, Clay, I know that what the Megis shell offers is worth its weight in diamonds, probably even more because it can literally prolong life. In that regard, Rex Trammer was smart to try and obtain it. But, in my heart I know that if we release the Megis shell into the world, our teachings and the culture of our Anishinaabe ancestors and our Chippewa nation will never be the same. As a people we'll be diminished because the power of the Megis shell will be abused by greedy opportunists. It's not a point I care to argue because I know the ways of the Light-Skinned race, and I know that I'm right. Having said that, I do believe there's merit in letting the world know that Brockway Mountain is home to a magnificent array of cave paintings and other ancient artifacts that can contribute much to the field of Anthropology and elevate the stature of our Chippewa people in the public's mind. If we successfully find our way out from under the mountain, there are some things we can reveal, but my friend, with all due respect, disseminating knowledge of the full power of the Megis shell is not one of them."

I listen to Robert's words and honestly can't convincingly counter anything he's said. "I understand," I reply to him. "From the little bit that we've seen of the shell's power, though, it seems like such a waste not to share it with people of good faith who will perish without its healing capabilities."

"Perhaps," Robert acknowledges. "My people and I continue to debate this very issue," but he declines to add further commentary. We continue our trek. Two hours pass, and it's clear that we are nearly spent. It's been well over twenty-four hours since Rex and Digger sealed Kelli and Rennie inside the Brockway Mine. Kelli stumbles on a rock in the path and says, "Can we rest a little? I'm worn out, Robert."

"Of course we can, but only for a little bit, Kelli, I sense great danger yet to come." He reaches into a deerskin pouch he carries in his belt and says,

"Here, each of you should chew these herbs. It'll provide a temporary boost of energy, but then we need to move on."

"What is it?" Rennie inquires.

"It's a special mixture that Nokomis taught me about in my youth. Chew it, but don't swallow it. It's very powerful."

We each do as he says, and Robert takes some for himself and gives a taste to Grey. Almost instantly we feel renewed energy and marvel at the inexplicable healing power of these native plants.

We continue walking another hour, and Robert holds his hand up and stops on the path. We are near the exit, but I sense great danger. "Grey, go ahead and scout the path before us, then return." The great grey wolf leaps ahead and is gone from view in a matter of seconds.

"What is it?" I ask Robert. "Is it the Windigo again?"

"Yes, but the evil one has recovered from your fight with him, and I sense that he's even larger and stronger than before."

"How's that possible?" Kelli asks.

"You must remember, Kelli, that the Windigo is also part spirit, and over many years it's adapted into a clever force. Much the same way that we Midewin healers have increased our knowledge, this cunning beast has learned as well."

"So, just how old is the Windigo?" Kelli asks.

"No one knows for sure, but perhaps as old as time itself. There are many good forces in the world, but they've always been countered by forces of evil. The Windigo is the embodiment of that evil, and we Midewin healers have been the only ones to keep it from wiping our people from the face of the earth. Our fear has always been that it will permanently leave the darkness of its underground realm and devour mankind and the forces of good. And now, it's growing in strength!"

"I don't understand, Robert, why is it that most people have never even heard of the Windigo before?" I ask.

"Because it's as I just said. The Windigo is very clever. We Chippewa have always known that, and long ago when white Europeans first settled this land, we tried to warn them, but we were dismissed as a bunch of backward Indians. The Windigo used this arrogant ignorance to its advantage and has bided its time, patiently waiting until it was ready."

"Oh swell!" Rennie inserts. "What can we do about it?"

"Yeah, Robert, what can we do about it? My Demon camera stopped it last time, but its power has been drained, and there's nothing down here to recharge it."

"Oh really?" Robert replies. "May I see your Demon device?"

I pull it out and hand it to him, and Kelli asks, "What is that thing? It looks like it's over a hundred years old."

"It is," I tell her. "It's from my antique camera museum, and some friends of mine modified it into a killer stun gun a number of years ago. I keep it close at hand for, uh, special occasions."

"Rennie, do I even want to know what he means by 'special occasions'?"

"Uh, probably not."

Robert examines it closely and closes his eyes. When he reopens them, he emits a bright ray of light at the Demon. Several moments later it glows with renewed energy. "I think you'll find it useful now," Robert advises matter-of-factly.

"Seriously?!" I reply. "Wow, you're like the Energizer bunny, thanks!"

Robert leads us forward on the trail keeping a careful eye out for the Windigo. Grey has not returned yet, and Robert views that as a possible sign that the Windigo may be further away from them than he'd thought. We soon come to a place that sends shivers down all of our spines. Off to the side of the trail in a tall, recessed cave we see a ten-foot high pile of bones. We walk over to examine the mound and recoil in shock when we see that the majority of the bones appear to be human, many of them quite old.

"Not a happy sight," I say sadly. "Not good at all, Robert."

"No," he agrees. "Definitely not what anyone wants to see. I fear that both of my parents lost their lives to the evil beast and their bones are probably scattered in this pile. Many of our people went missing when they collected copper ore from the caves."

"I'm very sorry, my friend," I say somberly.

"So, you see, defeating the evil, man-eating spirit is not only something that we must do for the outside world. It's something deeply personal to me and Nokomis."

I lightly place my hand on his shoulder. "We stick together on this, Robert. You and I both know it's our only way out. And, by the way, where's Nokomis?"

Robert smiles. "Grandmother? She's around somewhere. She's a mystery all right. You just never know when she's gonna appear … or disappear. Nokomis has been that way all of my life."

"Speaking of which, do you mind my asking how old you are?"

"No, I don't mind you asking, Clay, if you think you can handle the answer."

I look at him quizzically, and reply, "My honest impression is that you're both quite a mystery, plus we might as well add Grey to the mix, too. So, how old are you, really?"

Robert looks me directly in the eye and sighs, "Next spring I'll be 509 years old."

"No shit! I swear you don't look a day older than five hundred! Seriously, how old are you?"

"C'mon, Clay, let's keep going, and keep your Demon camera handy."

Chapter 20

Before long we leave the area of high ceilings, cascading waterfalls, and human bones to a tunnel leading gradually upward. It's not a steep slope, but given how weary we are, even a slight grade is noticeable. I look at Rennie and Kelli who're managing to keep pace and can't help but think that this is an experience that'll bond them forever. It's not unlike my friendship with Banks given all we experienced together saving Bodie and

Jake Horvath from the Russian thugs. I imagine that if we all live to tell about it, Robert and I will also feel a special bond.

We continue walking up the slope, and suddenly Robert raises his hand signaling for us to stop. A moment later Grey rejoins us, and Robert kneels down to meet his eyes. No words are spoken, but it's clear that they're communicating.

"The good news is that Grey has found our exit. The bad news is that the Windigo is asleep blocking it."

"How far?" I ask.

"A few hundred yards. Then there's a shallow stone wall we'll need to break through. Then sunlight and freedom."

His words are music to our ears, well at least the part about freedom and sunlight. As we prepare for this final leg in our struggle, I think about Maggie, Tori, and Mace. They have no idea what Rennie and I've been through since we last spoke. I'm not ready to die under this mountain, but if Rennie and I don't return, it saddens me greatly to think that they'll never know what had become of us. I look at Rennie and smile as I see him trying to encourage Kelli. He's such a fine young man, and I love having him as my son. We have to make it out of here.

Before long a putrid stench hits us, and we all know what that means. Robert signals for us all to be very quiet, and he motions for Rennie and Kelli to stay where they are while he, Grey, and I sneak forward. We peer around a large stone wall and see the hulking shape of the Windigo sleeping. It is one big, ugly, smelly, snoring, snorting beast.

"What now?" I ask Robert, and again he motions for complete silence. He knows we have just one shot at getting past the Windigo and out of the mine alive. Robert kneels down by Grey again and softly strokes his spirit guide. They seem to be communicating telepathically, planning a strategy on what to do next. Their bond is heartwarming.

Robert puts his finger to his lips signaling total silence as he motions for the three of us to come from behind the wall and stand six-feet abreast thirty feet in front of the slumbering beast. I'm scared shitless, especially because I know that Robert and Grey are deeply concerned as well.

Robert stands in the middle with Grey and me on either side of him. I watch him as he closes his eyes, presumably conjuring all he's learned from the Megis shell. When he reopens them there is a regal aura surrounding him, and he begins to softly chant incantations in a language I don't recognize. Grey paws at the soil, and the hackles on his back rise in furry spikes. He momentarily bears his fearsome teeth and looks at Robert for his command. They're ready to do battle, and like I said, I'm totally scared shitless.

All of a sudden the Windigo's eyes open, and now there's no turning back. The evil, man-eating beast stands on its huge, mole-like appendages and hurls a blood-curdling bellow in our direction. It's a fearsome sound, and the volume of Robert's incantations rises to meet it. The mole-bear-beast stands on its oversized feet and appears even taller than before. It growls and snarls ferociously, spewing sheets of rancid slobber onto the ground.

I watch as Robert closes his eyes and then a white-hot beam of light shoots from his forehead into the beast's neck. It recoils in pain and fright and attempts to steady itself.

"Grey, attack!" Robert shouts, and his spirit guide launches itself at the Windigo with terrifying ferocity. Grey literally scrambles up the Windigo's large, meaty right leg and clamps onto the evil beast's throat where Robert's beam had struck it moments ago. Despite the beast's shaking his head violently, he can't throw Grey from its neck. The Windigo attempts to bang Grey against the stone floor, but the huge canine hangs on like a savage warrior. The beast wails like a banshee and then slams Grey against the stone wall, and the heroic canine falls to the ground.

I look at Robert, and he quickly nods his head at me. The Demon camera is set to kill, and I discharge a lethal bolt of electricity at the same point in its neck that Robert and Grey had targeted. The Windigo slumps to its front knees attempting to protect itself from the deadly bolt. It wails in anguish and then charges me. I'm caught off guard at first and then run for the shelter of a nearby boulder. The beast smashes into the large boulder, and it cracks in half leaving me exposed.

Robert sees my vulnerability and casts another one of his cosmic, supercharged rays into the Windigo's hind quarters which pisses it off even more. It turns to face Robert, and I run in the other direction and check the Demon's battery charge. I see that I have one, maybe two more discharges before it's drained.

Now, we have a standoff. The Windigo's sixth sense tells it that it can beat this bothersome human, and it begins a slow walk in Robert's direction. I discharge the Demon a second time aiming it where I believe the beast's heart would be, and it crashes to the ground, wounded. Robert draws closer to the nasty creature for a coup de gras blast, and the Windigo charges at him again, knocking him to the ground, standing over him bellowing its imminent victory. I try the Demon one last time, and the cobalt blue stream of electricity ravages the Windigo's face. It lurches away from Robert and comes for me. I'm know I'm done and await my death. Rennie screams from the the side, "Daaaddd!" and his voice momentarily distracts the beast. "Hey ugly!" Rennie hollers at the Windigo. "You wanna a piece of Rennie Cotton, you big hairy rodent! Come and get me!"

I swear I see what looks like a satanic grin form on the Windigo's charred face as it leaves me and starts a slow, lumbering waddle toward my son. "Run, Rennie, run!" I scream, and he bolts for safety behind the wall where Kelli's hiding. Robert manages to recover a little and kneels facing the beast. He sends another of his searing blasts at the Windigo, and it appears to weaken it, but Robert's power has been weakened too. Robert calls to Grey, but the large canine is hurt and whimpers in pain. I run to Robert's side and help him to his feet. The Windigo turns to face us, leers menacingly, and rumbles its singed girth in our direction.

"Well, I guess this is it," I say to Robert, "Unless you've got another magic weapon I don't know about." He remains silent and closes his eyes for the beast's final assault.

The Windigo closes to within ten feet of us and grunts triumphantly. Then his haughty grunts turn to a horrific wail of pain as Robert and I see it consumed in a reddish-gold aura of burning light. Nokomis stands on a rock ledge above our battleground directing her deadly charge at the evil, man-eating spirit. It bellows and stomps as if trying to shed itself of Nokomis's lethal charge, but finally succumbs to the ancient woman's attack and literally explodes into putrid smelling atoms of vile nothingness. It's gone!

Robert and I are speechless as Nokomis floats down from the ledge and joins us. Rennie and Kelli come running from their hiding place and join us, equally stunned by what we all just witnessed.

"Nokomis!" Robert cries as he embraces his grandmother. "You saved us. You defeated the Windigo. We're alive because of you."

"Grey!" she says to Robert. "We must tend to your wolf pup before it's too late." We all walk over to Grey, and Robert and his grandmother fall to their knees on either side of their fallen friend. Nokomis pulls herbs from a deerskin pouch and places them on Grey's head and by his heart. Together, they place their hands on the great canine and lowly chant sacred Midewin incantations. Long seconds go by, and then Grey finally opens his eyes and stares at Robert.

"There you are, my friend, I thought we'd lost you." Tears roll down his cheeks, and he looks heavenward privately giving thanks to Manitou for the return on his spirit guide.

"Thank you, grandmother. Thank you for helping to bring him back to me." Robert embraces her again, and then he cries in a way that she remembers from long, long ago.

The five of us gather around Grey as he slowly regains his stability and stands. Not much is said by any of us at first. The combination of shock, utter fright, exhaustion, and unexpected victory is mind-numbing. We all hug each other instead, and not one of us is able to contain our tears of joy.

Robert and I look at each other with deep, abiding friendship. "Now I know what our friend, Banks, saw in you, Clay. I'd go into battle with you any day. Thank you, my friend." He places his hand on my heart, and I sense an enduring spiritual bond form.

"Oorah that!" I say repeating a marine battle cry that I learned from our mutual friend, Banks, in another time and place.

"Oorah that!" He replies with a broad smile. Nokomis looks on with maternal satisfaction.

"So," Robert asks. "Are any of you guys ready to get out from under this mountain?"

Cheers of affirmation erupt from each of us. He and Grey lead us to a stone wall that looks like all of the others, and he closes his eyes. We expect to see him cast an explosive white beam of light at the wall, but instead it begins to dematerialize leaving small pebbles and dusty sand at our feet. Robert leads us through the darkness, but this time we emerge and see stars, and our hearts soar. We're finally out.

Rennie turns to Ranger Kelli and smiles. "And, we lived to tell about it!" She gives him a warm hug of friendship and gratitude.

"Yeah, we lived to tell about it, Rennie!"

I turn to the group and say, "I only have one question. Actually, I really have a gazillion questions, but first, where the hell are we?"

Everyone laughs because we're just happy to finally be above ground. Robert says, "I think we're very close to the shoreline of Lake Superior near Copper Harbor. Not far from where my parents' Chippewa village was when I was a boy." Robert looks at Nokomis who nods her agreement.

"I don't suppose you've got Uber around here," I joke. "Didn't think so." We begin walking and finally arrive on the outskirts of town. It's very late and the town is dark. We walk down to a park at Lake Superior's edge and lie down on our backs to sleep. I stare up at the night sky and see a shooting star blaze across the night sky and turn to comment to Nokomis, but she's gone. I look at Robert, and he just shrugs and returns my surprised expression with a mirthful smile.

Chapter 21

THE NEXT DAY WE wake up early, dew-soaked and sore. We walk into town and enter Zik's diner and proceed to chow down on whatever we want … pancakes, omelets, home fries, toast, sausage, bacon, coffee. You name it. If it didn't move, we ate it. Kelli jokes with Rennie about their idea to start a cricket snack food company. "I'm game!" he says.

We go to pay, and I see Rennie reach into his pocket for cash but pulls out a couple of stones

instead. Kelli does the same and says to Robert, "I suppose you'll be wanting these diamonds back. We found them along the way."

I'm surprised to see what they have, but Robert says, "I know, but given everything that you've been through and what we survived, I think you deserve far more than that. Please keep them. And, I have a few thoughts I'd like to discuss with you later."

None of us are quite sure what he means, and in the meantime I just say, "The breakfast tab's on me."

I pay the bill, and we manage to snag a ride with an old coot of a guy in his hay wagon, and I'm happy to travel at a relaxed pace. The winding road up Brockway Mountain is lined with tall pines, birches, and maples trees that are soothing to my eyes. I'm so glad to be back in daylight; grateful to be alive, and to be able to enjoy this wondrous, natural scenery. Eventually, the old guy deposits us back at the main shaft house of the Brockway Mine. Digger Finn meets the wagon not knowing that we're passengers and damn near micturates himself when we get out to confront him.

"Hello, Digger, got time for a mine tour?" I ask caustically. He tries to run, but Rennie tackles him a few feet away.

"But how'd you …" he starts to blurt and then says, "Don't hurt me. I was just following orders from my boss."

"Uh huh!" Kelli says. "You two tried to kill us, you bastard!"

Robert glares at the pitiful man with contempt and asks, "Where's your boss, Digger? The hospital?"

He stares at the ground and shakes his head yes.

"And where's my Jeep, Digger? I left it right over there."

"And where's my Subaru, you jerk?!" Kelli piles on.

Digger mumbles something unintelligible and Robert presses him again. "Where are our vehicles?"

"Uh, I got rid of them earlier today. Sold 'em for scrap."

"Oh, so you wanted to get rid of the evidence the same way you wanted to bury each of us, right?"

"I told you I was just following orders," he feebly replies.

"The Cadillac Escalade, Digger. Give me the keys."

Digger reaches in his pocket and pulls out the keys. "You can expect a visit from the police later today, Digger. I don't suggest that you try to run either because I think you know that information has a way of flowing to me. I'll easily find you, and given the hateful things you and Rex did to us, you're seeing my charitable mood now. Don't test me, Digger."

As if to punctuate Robert's admonition, Grey walks over and urinates on Digger's pant leg.

———

The scenic drive back to Calumet from Brockway Mountain is subdued. We drive past the ghost towns of Mandan, Delaware, Central, and Phoenix, and I can't help but wonder if the Windigo killed miners all along the Keweenaw Peninsula's rocky spine. We talk sporadically among ourselves, but each of us also spends alone time just staring out the car window. It was a horrible experience that none of us will ever forget, but the good news is that we came through it together.

"Where to, Kelli?" Robert asks as we approach Calumet. "Your apartment?"

"Yeah," she replies. "I could use a hot shower and some clean sheets. Will I see you at the office tomorrow, Rennie?" she asks.

"Yeah, you can count on me, Ranger Kelli. We've got a lot of stuff to sort through, don't we?"

"And," Robert adds. "Once we all get ourselves resettled, I think the four of us need to spend time together talking about what we share with the public and how we disseminate it."

We drop Kelli off at her apartment which is in easy walking distance to her office at the National Park Service. It's emotionally hard for her to say goodbye to us, but she gets out of the backseat and gives us a wan smile. Rennie watches as she climbs the steps to her front door and feels a sense of relief that she's finally safe at home.

"You know, Dad, she really was rock solid under the mountain, and I learned a lot by seeing how well she dealt with adversity. In the end, we were darn lucky to have each other, otherwise I doubt either of us would've survived."

I squeeze Rennie's shoulder. "I'm glad you came up to the Keweenaw this summer, son, not that I want you to ever experience anything like we did, but having survived it, it's the kind of experience that nobody can ever take away from you."

Robert looks at Rennie in the rearview mirror and tells him they'll talk soon. He then drives a couple of blocks and deposits us in front of Rennie's apartment. Thankfully, I see that Pappy is still parked where I left it.

"Thanks!" I say to Robert as we exit the Escalade. "Seriously, Robert, thanks for bringing us through a terrifying life-and-death experience."

"You too, Clay. We made it because we all stuck together."

"So, where're you and Grey heading now? Back to Baraga?"

"Yeah," he says, "but first I need to visit someone in the hospital and then talk with the police."

"What do you think will happen to Rex Trammer and Digger Finn?"

"Well, the courts will be the final arbiter of justice, but given Rex's poor prognosis, the courts will likely let nature take its course. I doubt Trammer will ever serve any serious jail time. There's justice either way. As for Digger, well, I think he can expect to be a 'guest' at a federal prison for a number of years."

"Suits me just fine."

Rennie looks at Robert, and solemnly says, "Sir, I can't tell you how grateful I am to you and your grandmother, and Grey, for saving us. And, I want you to know that I'm totally awestruck by the cave paintings and other artifacts that we saw. The history and culture of your people, its very early roots, its rich belief systems … they're all very special. In my opinion the artwork exceeds any ethnographic cave art in North America and possibly the world. Aside from being scared out of my wits 90 percent of the time, I'm really proud to have experienced this with you."

"Thank you, Rennie, you certainly proved yourself down there, my friend, and you're welcome among our people any time."

We say goodbye for now to Robert and prepare to go inside Rennie's apartment to call Maggie and then crash.

"What are we gonna say to mom?" he asks me. "Anything? Everything?"

"Darned if I know, son, but the less said is probably better. What do you think?"

"Probably. She already freaks whenever you plan to travel somewhere."

"Tell me about it," I say, "but you have to remember that I've given her plenty of reasons to get freaked!"

"Point taken."

We head inside, and I call Maggie. "Hi sweetheart, how're things at home?" I ask benignly.

"Clay, there you are! I was wondering when I was going to hear from you guys. I take it you and Rennie have been up to a lot of excitement, hopefully nothing like the time you guys went to Dead Horse Point in Utah."

"Yeah, it's been action-packed, that's for sure. Sorry I've been out of contact, but Rennie, his supervisor, Kelli, and I have been doing some, uh, spelunking in Brockway Mountain."

"Sounds a little creepy to me. Did you find anything interesting?"

"Yeah, we did as a matter of fact. We came across an incredible section with ancient Indian cave paintings. Rennie seems to think they're as important as anything discovered to date. He may be helping curate the find."

"Wow, that's impressive!" Maggie chirps. "Is my son available to talk with me?"

"Sure," I say. "He's right here."

I hand the phone to Rennie, and he nods at me indicating he won't tell her about the really frightening stuff.

"Hi Mom, how're you doing?"

"I'm fine. Tori's fine. We sure miss you. How's work and are you enjoying some great adventures?"

"Yeah, work's good. Just trying to keep from getting buried under the, uh, workload. How's Mace getting along?"

"He's struggling more these days, but heck he's in his late eighties after all. I can tell he misses you a lot. So, when are you coming home?"

"Well, I'm not exactly sure. I heard Dad tell you about our finding the fascinating cave paintings. Since I found them with Ranger Kelli, we may be working on them together for a little while yet. I need to tell my academic advisor about our find, and given its significance I'm sure he'll let me extend my internship up here. It's been quite an experience so far, that's for sure."

The three of us talk for a few minutes longer, then hang up, and Rennie and I exhale sighs of relief that we got through our conversation with Maggie without having to reveal details about the truly terrifying episodes.

"I sure hate being so oblique with your mom about what we've experienced, but …" We both know there's nothing to be gained from being totally transparent.

"I'm really bushed, Dad. Do you mind if I crash?"

"No, son, go ahead. I'm exhausted too. I want you to know that I'm very proud of the way you handled yourself under the mountain. Life's certainly a mystery sometimes, isn't it?"

He nods his agreement. "How do you explain Robert, Nokomis, Grey, and the Windigo to someone who wasn't there?"

"Darned if I know. I'm still can't believe what happened. I'll see you in the morning, Rennie. Let's hope we both have sweet dreams without any monsters."

Rennie shuffles off to bed, and I retire to his den to do the same. As exhausted as I am, I have trouble falling asleep at first. My brain keeps doing a mental inventory of things that we saw, experienced, and survived. I'm a guy approaching fifty years of age now, and I've had many fascinating and frightening experiences, but nothing that compares with what I've witnessed on Brockway Mountain and the Keweenaw Peninsula. I mean, a Chippewa Indian leader, his grandmother, and a wolf that can divine things that aren't humanly possible, or artwork and diamonds and minerals beyond the wealth of King

Midas, and of course, the evil Windigo. I mean, holy shit! There's a reason I'm having trouble falling asleep, but eventually I do, and I sleep as deeply and as peacefully as I've ever done before.

Chapter 22

THE NEXT DAY PASSES rather uneventfully which is a welcome relief to say the least. While Rennie is at work, I take the opportunity to get to know the Keweenaw Peninsula a little better. I drive back through a few of the ghost towns and photograph whatever catches my eye. I'd be lying if I didn't say I looked over my shoulder more than once expecting someone like Nokomis to show up, but she didn't materialize.

The coastal towns I drive through like Copper Harbor, Eagle Harbor, and Eagle River are charming with their quaint buildings, rock-strewn beaches, and lighthouses. I snap pictures just like any other tourist. Thankfully, my photography brings me a feeling of calmness like very few things can, and I relax seeing what I frame in my viewfinder.

Being alone on the road gives me plenty of time to think, and more than anything I think about how much I miss Maggie and our close family of friends. Surviving what we did helps me put the meaning of life in perspective, not that I wasn't already aware, but I'm definitely ready to return home once Robert, Kelli, Rennie, and I have our final confabulation.

As for Rennie, he got up early the day after we returned from Brockway Mountain and met Kelli in the office. Her supervisor stops by and asks where they'd been, and Kelli asks her to step inside her office. She closes the door and says, "Please sit down, Glenda. Rennie and I have a story to tell you."

Over the next thirty minutes Kelli and Rennie share details about driving to Copper Harbor and Brockway Mountain looking for information that residents might have about the mysterious Megis shell. She tells her about their visit with Thomas Arrowsmith, and then stopping by the Brockway Mining Company to interview Rex Trammer.

Ranger Glenda is appalled when she hears that Rex and Digger had entombed them under the mountain in order to try to trade them for the Megis shell, and she nearly faints when they tell her about the incredible discovery of Paleo-Indian art. Kelli also tells her how Robert Midew and Rennie's father, Clay Arnold, had found them but had gotten trapped themselves when Digger blew up the mine's entrance. The only things that Kelli and Rennie don't tell her about are Robert and Nokomis's mysterious sorcery, the vast wealth of minerals they'd discovered, and the evil, man-eating-spirit, Windigo. She and Rennie had agreed that permission to speak of those things should only be given by Robert.

"So, how'd you all get out?" is Glenda's immediate question.

"Robert Midew knew of a separate opening," Kelli fibs, "and we eventually crawled out."

"And, what about calling the police on Trammer and this Digger guy?" Glenda asks.

"Robert's already taken care of that."

"So, what do you want to do next?" Glenda asks.

"Well, we need to talk more with Robert since this is clearly his peoples' history, but Glenda, the world won't believe the cave art that Rennie and I found. It'll change the way we think about Chippewa culture. We could study this find for years and still have plenty to research. I would very much like for

Rennie and me to do extensive research on the site and prepare a comprehensive study of our findings. Believe me, we won't have any difficulty finding funding for this."

"Well, obviously I'm stunned, and I must say very proud of both of you. I'll talk with my superiors also, but I agree that if what you describe is the real thing, then I would love for you guys to handle the research. You'll get a lot of well-deserved credit for this. Oh, and what about the Megis shell that's gotten everyone here and in Washington all hot and bothered?"

"Well, that's a subject that the park service's higher-ups are going to have to discuss with Robert and the tribal council," Kelli replies. "Rennie and I are expecting a call from him soon to schedule a time for us to meet, so as hard as it might be for you, we'd like to ask you to keep it among us until we meet with Robert."

Glenda smiles, "It'll be very tough, but I think I can do that. Good going, guys! Rennie, how's this for an internship so far?!" she asks playfully. "Wow, prehistoric Native American art right here in the Keweenaw!" Glenda mumbles incoherent babble to herself and giggles as she exits Kelli's office and closes the door.

Kelli and Rennie smile at each other and continue working on a stack of education requests from area schools. An hour later Kelli's phone rings, and she sees that it's Robert calling.

"Greetings, sir!" she chirps. "Wanna go for a walk under a mountain?!"

"Not today, Kelli, it sounds dark and dank and filled with spooky things," he teases back. "I'm calling to touch base with you and Rennie, and I'll give Clay a call after we hang up. After dealing with Rex Trammer and the police, I convened a meeting of our Chippewa tribal council. I gave our members a full, unvarnished account of what had occurred at Brockway Mountain, including the art and mineral discoveries and our battle with the Windigo. All of our members were thunderstruck by what I shared with them. We had a frank discussion that went late into the night, and we've made some decisions. I'd like for the two of you and Clay to come to our council meeting this evening for you to share your accounts and to hear what we've decided. Will you please convey this to Rennie too?"

"I sure will, Robert. In fact, he's standing right here with me now."

"Good, then we'll see the three of you here at the tribal center around seven o'clock."

"We'll be there for sure. I know we're all looking forward to it. Thanks, Robert." They hang up.

A few minutes before seven Kelli, Rennie, and I arrive in the town of Baraga at the base of the Keweenaw Peninsula. Kelli directs us to the tribal council headquarters, and I park Pappy in a spot marked for visitors. We exit the truck and see Robert waiting for us at the entrance. He's smiling but also has a solemn look on his face.

He leads us inside the modern building, and we enter a spacious meeting room that's decorated with Chippewa artifacts showcasing their tribe's culture spanning many centuries. I can see that Rennie is spellbound by the colorful array of ethnographic examples: Tools and weapons, headdresses, cradleboards, beaded garments, and puckered moccasins. I wish I had my camera with me, but we're clearly here for a different reason.

There are six people already seated around the council table. Their smiles and handshakes are friendly, but like Robert, they also exude a solemn bearing. Robert introduces us and asks each of the council members to introduce themselves as well. Robert's friend, Willow, is present as is Tommy Two-Feathers. Grey lies quietly in the corner of the room watching and listening.

"Where to begin?" Robert asks rhetorically. He tells us that he's already shared vivid details about what we witnessed and endured under Brockway Mountain with the council members, and he invites us to offer our versions as well.

Rennie and I look to Kelli to begin. "First, my friends and I wish to thank you very much for inviting us to your center. I'm sure that Robert has conveyed stunning details about what we saw and endured. We can assure you that there's no exaggeration regarding the incredible Chippewa artwork and valuable minerals that we found, and to be sure, the description of our struggle against the terrifying Windigo. Frankly, we're all fortunate to be alive today. If it weren't for our sticking together, and having the fortuitous sudden appearance of Nokomis, we would all be dead."

Murmurs are heard around the table, and we see heads nodding respectful understanding.

Tommy Two-Feathers says, "You've witnessed things that none of us have ever seen. We've heard stories that most of us thought were colorful myths about great wealth and ferocious beasts, but your affirmation of what Robert has told us will forever change what we believe among our people. We're very grateful for what you've shared."

"My son, Rennie, and I can also assure you that what you've heard is true," I add. "We were all mere seconds away from death on more than one occasion."

Over the next several minutes we receive and answer questions from members of the tribal council's board. No official minutes are taken by the council's secretary. No written account of our conversations and testimonies is preserved. This frank and open discussion is for eyes and ears only. We continue speaking among ourselves a little while longer, and once Robert is satisfied that each individual has had ample opportunity to listen and be heard, he addresses us.

"My friends, this is a momentous time, and what our tribal council has decided will help preserve the sanctity and honor of our Chippewa people and our Anishinaabe ancestors going forward. Each of us knows the reasonable arguments for sharing the life-saving secrets of our sacred Megis shell with the rest of the world. Each of us also knows the dire consequences of giving this powerful information away to people who would praise us with words, and yet abuse this newly found power with avarice and control. It is therefore our decision NOT to share the power of the Megis shell with the world, and similarly we've decided against publicly announcing the discovery of great wealth under the mountain or the very existence of the evil Windigo. To do so would only encourage unwelcome intruders who would ravage the sacred mountain."

"Kelli, Clay, and Rennie, you have our heartfelt gratitude for all that you've endured, and also for the respect and deference you've shown to our Chippewa ways. We hope you understand and can accept our decisions."

Robert looks around the table at each face and continues, "There is so much to be learned from the cave paintings and other ancient artifacts under Brockway Mountain. It's our collective hope that Kelli and Rennie, with my assistance as needed, will assiduously study and document this great cache of historic art. Clay, if you're willing, we would greatly appreciate your photographing this find and having your photographs provide the visual documentation. The integrity of your fame will lend further credibility. Perhaps you would consider returning to the Keweenaw Peninsula in a few weeks to begin your work. Rest assured, whatever financial resources the three of you require will be made available by our Chippewa treasury. In that way our people will be beholden to no one from the outside because of financial investment."

I look at Robert and the tribal council members and say, "It would be my honor to help in any way you want. We can discuss specifics later."

Kelli and Rennie are delighted that they've earned the trust of the tribal council as well and echo similar sentiments. "Rennie and I assure you," Kelli says, "that we'll conduct our studies and what we eventually write with utmost professionalism and respect. We thank you for giving us this important responsibility."

Finally, the meeting comes to an end, and the council members gradually drift from the council chamber. While Kelli and Rennie visit with Grey, Robert calls me aside and says, "My friend, I have some things for you." He hands me a heavy deer-skin sack and says, "Here are a few, uh, baubles for Rennie and Kelli to use as they see fit. Please divide these diamonds between them and give the stones to them before you return home. I do not wish to embarrass them now."

"Are you serious, Robert, these gemstones are worth thousands if not millions of dollars," I say with shock. He smiles back at me warmly.

I turn to leave, and Robert says, "Wait, Clay, there's something else that I have for you, but I give it to you on one condition."

"Oh!?" I say.

Robert hands me a modest-looking wooden box and says, "I want you and your family to have this, but I want you to only open it in the presence of your family of friends when you return home. Will you please agree to that?"

I look at Robert appreciatively, not having a clue to the box's contents and shake my head in agreement. "I promise, Robert, thank you in advance for whatever your gift is. I'll call you from home, and we can schedule my return visit."

We join Rennie, Kelli, and Grey to say good night, and the three of us then exit the tribal council headquarters and climb back into Pappy for the return drive to Calumet.

Along the way, I toss the deerskin sack to Kelli and casually say, "Here! Robert wants the two of you to equally divide what's inside. He says you've earned it!"

Kelli and Rennie peer inside the sack and aren't sure whether to laugh or cry, and so they do both. "He did say that he prefers that you keep this as our little secret."

"Not a problem!" they both say in unison.

The rest of the thirty-minute drive is quiet with the occasional sound of hoots and hollers. Given everything that's happened over the last few days, it's about as eloquent a collection of sounds as you can imagine. We drop Kelli at her apartment near the park service, and I say goodbye for now. Rennie walks her to her door, and I see them give each other fond hugs. He returns a moment later, and I steer Pappy back toward his apartment. We're both basking in a heartwarming glow.

I watch Rennie as he stares vacantly out of his passenger window, and I suddenly notice a surprised expression come on his face. I say, "Rennie, what's the matter, son, you look like you've just seen a ghost!"

He turns to me and says, "Wow, for a second there, Dad, I thought I did, but it was only an old Indian woman walking along the side of the road with a young boy and a wolf pup."

Epilogue

T HE NEXT MORNING I get up early, and Rennie and I share breakfast together before he prepares to head to the park service to begin a new day. I'm delighted that he has a spring in his step, and that he's excited about life, not to mention just being alive. I have a good feeling that his experiences

this summer will help propel his doctoral can-
didacy and hopefully his career. We go over our
calendars together and tentatively pick some dates
for my return to begin photographing the cave art,
depending on Robert's schedule too.

I load my gear into Pappy and carefully pack
the box that Robert gave me on the passenger's
seat. True to my word, I haven't peeked inside and
promise myself not to do so until I'm with Maggie,
Tori, and Mace. Besides, knowing Robert's unique
talent for having information flow to him, I figure
it's better not to risk it.

Rennie and I say goodbye for now, and I steer
Pappy onto U.S. Route 41 heading west along the
spine of the Keweenaw Peninsula through Hancock,
Houghton, and Baraga. From there I turn south
along the eastern side of Wisconsin. It'll be a long,
ten-hour drive back home, perhaps even longer
depending on the traffic around Milwaukee and
Chicago, and I settle in for the drive and listen to
one of my favorite Weed Rawlins CDs.

As I've mentioned before, being alone on the
road gives me ample opportunity to think about
all sorts of things, some great, some not-so-great,
and a bunch of stuff in between. Maggie's definitely
correct when she says I have a knack for getting
involved in some major shitstorms. This trip certainly ranked right up there at the top. I shake my

head in disbelief thinking about what I saw, experienced, and survived.

"Whew!" I exhale out loud to myself. "No one who wasn't there could ever possibly believe it."

A few hours pass, and I eventually drive through the Chicago area with typical slowdowns due to congested traffic and road repairs. I always have a feeling of relief when Chicago's in my rearview mirror, and I finally enter northern Indiana and the final leg of my journey. I stop for a late lunch in Merrillville and then drive the final two hours arriving home around five o'clock. It's hard to believe that it's only been about a week since I left home for Michigan because it feels like a lifetime.

Satchmo, our Maine Coon cat, comes scampering to meet me as I park Pappy, followed shortly thereafter by Maggie who I envelop in a tight hug. "Man, I missed you!" I say looking into those emerald green eyes I've come to adore.

"Me, too, sweeteheart! It's always a relief to have you home where you belong."

I see Tori come out to the front porch of the old farmhouse across the brick courtyard, and Mace manages to hobble out of his home in the old brewery complex's power plant. I can't begin to say how happy I am to be home with them.

"Welcome home, Clay!" Tori shouts. "I'd know the sound of that old truck any day! We all agreed that we'd come over to my place for some refreshments once you get settled, okay?"

"Thanks, Tori. Maggie and I'll catch up with you in a little bit after I stow my gear."

I see Mace beaming at me while he leans on an old post for support. "Always great to see you come back from some place in one piece, my friend."

I give him a knowing nod and say, "I tell you all about it later. It was a good trip, but there were moments when I had a demon of a time."

He catches my drift, and his eyebrows arch in expectation.

Maggie and I enter our home in the old brewery building with Satchmo in hot pursuit. We take the elevator two flights up to our bedroom, and Maggie helps me empty my stuff and tosses my used clothes down the laundry chute.

"So, what was that cryptic message you just voiced to Mace about a demon of a time? Did you and Rennie run into any trouble?"

"Naw, not really," I reply evenly. "Leastwise not something we couldn't handle, honey."

"That's all you're going to tell me, isn't it, Clay?"

"Yeah, for now, Maggie, and I could definitely use another hug."

"Well, you can have a little more than that, but then we should meet Mace and Tori at the farmhouse. We're all excited to have you home, and we want to hear about your adventures."

Maggie and I finish up stowing my stuff, and we take the elevator down to the courtyard.

"Hold on a second, honey," I say to her. "I need to get something out of Pappy."

I open the passenger side's door, and gently lift the old, carved, wooden box that Robert gave me when we parted company at the tribal council.

"Neat box!" Maggie exclaims. "What's in it?"

"I'm not sure. Robert Midew, who's the president of the Chippewa tribal council, gave it to me yesterday and asked me to wait to open it until I was home with you guys. Robert's a very, uh, unique man, so I'm anxious to see what's inside as well."

Mace and Tori are already seated around her dining table when we enter, and I take a seat next to Mace. Tori gets up and Maggie joins her to help serve refreshments.

"Demon of a time?!" Mace asks me with a look of surprise and concern etched on his face.

"The scariest ever!" And from my expression Mace sees that I'm not kidding. "We'll talk later."

Tori and Maggie sit down, and we make idle small talk for a few minutes. I love the mundanity of it all. It feels so good to be home.

"So, let's see what's in this box that Robert Midew gave me! He told me it was a thank-you gift." I explain who Robert is to them as I open the box and see a letter to me and three small deerskin pouches, each of which has a handwritten label on it for Maggie, Mace, and Tori. The letter has a tag that says, "Read me first!" I unfold it, and read it aloud.

>*"Dear Clay, it's hard for me to adequately express my gratitude to you, Rennie, and Kelli for all that you did for our Chippewa nation these last few days, and what you've all agreed to do with what we found. No one will ever truly know what we all experienced under Brockway Mountain, and I imagine that you agree it's better that we keep it that way.*
>
>*Given your collective sacrifice and your enduring friendship to me and my people, I have some gifts for your family of friends whom you and Rennie told me about. I know that they mean the world to you. I only suggest that you distribute each gift to Maggie, Mace, and Tori in order and follow my instructions. This is my gift to you, Clay. With my heartfelt thanks, Robert."*

I reach inside the box and pull out the pouch that has Maggie's name on it and give it to her. She feels its weight in her hand, unties its drawstring, and pulls out a stone the size of a very large hen's egg.

"It's a rock!" she exclaims. "Huh, that was very nice of him. I'll have to get a note of thanks off to him."

I see what it is and say, "Honey, you might want to take a look at it again. It's not just any rock."

She looks at me quizzically, and I say, "It's a huge, uncut diamond, Maggie, and knowing Robert, it's of exceptionally fine quality and possibly worth millions!"

She gulps. "Are you serious, Clay? Seriously, are you serious!"

I smile and nod yes.

I read Robert's next instructions in his letter and pull out the pouch with Mace's name on it and hand it to him.

"Hmmm," he ponders aloud. "It doesn't have the weight of a stone, so I guess I didn't get a diamond. In fact, it barely has any weight at all."

Mace opens the pouch, and I say, "Robert's instructions are that you put these herbs in your mouth but do not swallow them."

He's understandably confused by what these herbs will do, but he does as Clay says and places the herbs on his tongue and closes his mouth. Several seconds go by, and Mace shrugs his shoulders as if to say, "So?!" A few moments later he sits upright in his chair, spits out the herbs, stands, and proceeds to strut around like a happy rooster.

"Holy cow! I haven't felt this alive since the hogs ate brother!" he jokes. "Really everyone, I feel like I'm twenty years old!"

I privately read more of Robert's letter which says the effects of the herbs will boost Mace's health for several more years. I'm thrilled beyond words that we'll have Mace in our lives for longer than we'd expected. What a gift! Tori and Maggie are over-the-moon with happiness at Mace's revitalization. Robert has given us our friend back.

Finally, we come to Tori's sack, and I place it in her hands. Tori has been a lifelong friend who's been blind since birth. I love her like a sister, and Maggie, Mace, Rennie, Bodie, and I have always been happy to help her navigate her dark, sightless world. I only wish that her late brother, Weed, was still with us.

"It's soft," she comments about the deerskin pouch. "And light! I don't think I'm getting a diamond either, Mace."

I read Robert's instructions further and say aloud, "Robert wants you to tilt your head back while I place these herbs on your forehead, your heart, and your closed eyes.

Tori shifts down in her chair and tilts her head back. Maggie helps get her into a comfortable position, and I follow Robert's instructions precisely. I lightly sprinkle the herbs on Tori where Robert indicated. Several moments go by, and we soon see a golden glow envelop Tori's face and head. A look of astonishment appears on her face. She carefully wipes the herbs from her face, sits upright, and I see tears of joy cascade down her cheeks. She slowly peers at each of us as she's never done before and joyfully voices words none of us ever expected to hear, "I can see!"

~ The End ~

About the Author
Stuart Fabe

SINCE RETIRING FROM HIS professional career several years ago, Stuart Fabe has directed his creative energies to night sky photography and writing suspense novels. Over the last four decades, Stuart has also published six fine art photography books and exhibited his artwork and photographs at numerous art shows and galleries. His work is widely collected.

Copper Evening is Stuart's sixth novel and the fifth story in his Clay Arnold series. He enjoys the role of storyteller and in creating fascinating characters and compelling page-turning plots. His writing is intended solely as entertainment.

Stuart lives in the bucolic countryside near Greencastle, Indiana, with his partner, Marla Helton, two dogs, two cats, and nine hens.